The Summer After the Funeral

By Jane Gardam

A LONG WAY FROM VERONA
A FEW FAIR DAYS
THE SUMMER AFTER THE FUNERAL

The Summer
After the Funeral

Jane Gardam

MACMILLAN PUBLISHING CO., INC.
New York

First published in Great Britain
by Hamish Hamilton Children's Books Ltd

Macmillan Publishing Co., Inc., 866 Third Avenue, New York, N.Y. 10022

Library of Congress catalog card number: 73-4058

Printed in the United States of America

10 9 8 7 6 5 4 3 2 1

Library of Congress Cataloging in Publication Data

Gardam, Jane.   The summer after the funeral.

[1. England—Fiction]   I. Title.   PZ7.G163Su3   [Fic]   73-4058
ISBN 0-02-735880-1

For Stone

We are not free to choose by what we
shall be enchanted, truly or falsely.
In the case of a false enchantment
all we can do is take immediate flight
before the spell really takes hold.

W. H. Auden, *A Certain World*

Contents

PART ONE

July

Chapter One

"I thought Athene did very well," said Boo.

"Very well," said Mrs. Price, the widow. "They all did well."

"Sebastian—"

"Yes. But Sebastian has the warmest heart. The loftiness is all for cover."

"I do so adore Sebastian," said Boo. "Are you all right, Dodo?"

"Of *course*, my dear."

Mrs. Price stood in her drawing room in the bright afternoon sunshine waiting for the funeral guests to come in from the churchyard at the end of the garden. They were at present in groups under the lychgate, quiet and well turned out like their cars which were standing about the drive and the leafy lane beyond. They were leaving a decent interval for the widow and her sister to be together before the handing of teacups.

Throughout the service and during the stern words in the damp graveyard—rowdy rooks above—the old Rector's family had behaved like heroes. The widow, steady as a dwarf oak, had been clearly heard to make the Responses, seen to pat a hand upon a pew, at the door to kiss a cousin unnoticed earlier, even (surely not) as she moved away and through the rectory wicket home, even to take a quick glance at her watch, considering kettles.

"Dodo has gone home with Boo," people told each other with the solemn kindness that obtains at gravesides. They felt proud of her, proud to know her, excited by her confident, steady face. Unkind people might have felt it was a self-satisfied face, but kind ones—and for half an hour they were kind—saw only a face grateful to its Maker for an opportunity of proclaiming faith.

"And after all," they said, kind and unkind, as they lingered about the gravel, slowly drawing nearer to tea, "after all, the dear old boy must have been about ninety."

" 'Darling,' " said Beams, but nobody spoke.

" 'Darling, darling, darling,' " she said again. "They're all saying darling."

"Sometimes," said Sebastian after a while, "they're saying 'Where are the children?' Sybil Bowles came in. I was through the french window. 'Oh, Dodo, where are the children?' "

"Who's Sybil Bowles?"

"Godchild. Same age as Mother. Her eyes were bright red. She was mad about him."

"Was she the tall, narrow one with a little cloche hat?"

"Yes."

"With a head like a hen and one thick leg?"

"Yes."

4

"What did Ma say?"

"She said, 'Helping, Sybil dear,' and flung herself at the next one. Auntie Posie."

"Who?"

"Posie-Wosie, dear old Posie. She didn't have red eyes. She was beaming her head off. And looking round for the cakes."

"I've never seen Auntie Posie not beaming," said Beams.

"She ought to be you," said Sebastian. Beams was short for Moonbeams (Phoebe at the font) and referred to her great, flashing glasses. Beams was ugly, with the face of a frog—wide-mouthed, chinless, thin hair in palish wisps and a gooping expression. Twelve years old. Alas for her.

They were in the barn. You opened the tall doors and went through the carriage house where eighteenth-century rectors had kept horses and the Prices a battered car until the Rector gave up driving—their mother had not taken to motor cars. You then went up a ladder to the hayloft, which had a step in the middle, excellent for dividing stage from audience in concerts when they were little. There was a heap of hay at the back, and through the stone slits of the walls sunlight pierced with hay dust dancing in it, throwing great splashes of light on the boards. Beams sat doing something nasty to her fingernails in the hay. Sebastian leaned against the wall, his face turned sideways with a noble expression upon it. Their sister Athene stood at one of the stone slits looking upward, arching her long neck and stroking it.

"Posie Dixon," she said gently to the sky.

"Lord!" said Sebastian.

"Did you go in?" asked Beams.

"No."

"How did you see, then?"

"Well, I was going in."

After a long time he said, "I wasn't going in. I looked in. Through the french windows. Then I went away."

"Did they see you?"

"No. They're too busy. Having a good time."

Beams began picking little bits of hay from under her legs and chewing them, and Sebastian started sneezing. "Après-midi sur les herbes," he said. "Athene ought to have no clothes on."

"For goodness sake!" said Beams.

"Oh, sorry, pas devant les—"

Beams fell on him and kicked him. He held her off and laughed at her. She bit his wrist. He shouted and cuffed her head. She began to cry.

"Oh, hush," said Athene. "Do shut up. You're not children, for heaven's sake. Do hush." She stopped stroking her neck, but did not turn round.

Sebastian sucked his wrist and then brushed his trouser knees sideways briskly with the palm of his other hand. "Oh, come on, Beams," he said. "Where's your glasses?" He picked them up for her. "We'd better go over. You coming, Ath?"

"In a minute," she said. "Tell her I'm coming."

They waited about. "Don't be long," said her brother. "We ought to go over. She's funny—putting us through things. Not discussing. She *thinks* we'll go over."

"She knows we'll go over," said Beams. "She wants us to be admired."

Athene leaned her head against the stone and the other two went away. She watched them cross the stableyard beneath her, into the kitchen garden and through the raspberries. The trailing canes dragged at Sebastian's best dark suit. They passed out of sight behind feathers of asparagus. Two very clean tea towels hung side by side with dips in the middle on the line by the back kitchen door. A fat thrush sat on an iron post in the raspberries, so full of them that its beak dripped red juice. No one had netted the raspberries that summer.

"There are things not to be thought of," she said aloud in the barn. "There are words not to be said." The church clock struck four times slowly, but not so slowly as the bell before. It had been almost a relief then when that bell had started after the awful morning—the waking up to marvelous sunshine after a week of rain, the sparkling grass, Mother calling about, the phone ringing, extra milk, cutting the egg sandwiches thin enough. There'd been an awful row about Auntie Boo not cutting the egg sandwiches thin enough. And the getting ready, all clean and calm like for a queer party. For Buckingham Palace. And the following out. The front door, through the wicket, the humps of green, the flash of flowers, the tall black shadowy men with professional understanding faces presenting hymn books, white-handed. Like a Dickens film.

There are some thoughts not to be thought.

There was a ping-pong ball stuck in a crack—a demon shot of Seb's a year ago. She picked it out and flung it across the barn. It hit the wall, the rafters, the floor and vibrated away, making smaller and smaller noises, clear and urgent as though it were alive. Sounds never stop. They hang about forever, high in the sky, close to the flowering earth. Only matter vanishes, back to the earth from whence . . .

"Well now," she said, and set off after the others, slim and dark and calm (she was sixteen) across the yard, round into the front garden and the drive, determinedly past the churchyard gate and the shadow that might be the old sexton walking slowly in the sun, not turning her head, in through the great front door that stood wide open.

"Athene," they all cried, "Athie," "Ath," "Duckie," "Darling." All the parsons, the tea urn, the sandwiches, the flutter were a parish party, but dream-like, for all the clothes were black. And Sybil Bowles' red eyes brimmed over and Posie Dixon beamed.

Chapter Two

Athene Price was extraordinary. She was healthy, popular and good, happy at school, contented at home, effortlessly clever and played the piano like an angel. A fat, sweet-tempered baby, a very pretty small child, she had never been spoiled; an elder daughter, she had not grown bossy. She had been liked by her elder brother, not resented by her younger sister, was uncritical of her parents and adored the rectory and village that she lived in, yet she had gone sensibly off to boarding school at ten without tears. There she had grown out of childhood without spots or obesity or tantrums or silences, and, by the time she was sixteen, when she came into a room people generally felt the better for it.

She was a girl you remembered. Middle-aged males particularly would say, "Price? Aren't those the people with the daughter?" or "I must say it's worth going all the way to Newton Abbey to see that splendid girl."

For Athene lived up to her name. The thing about her more

extraordinary than anything else, the thing you could not deny or even question, whoever you were—Beams, for instance— was that she was a beauty. You could wonder at it, especially after a good look at the little brown mother and the ancient father with his long head and papery hands—but a beauty she was and, by the look of her bones and gigantic, calm eyes (there had been some great-grandmother from somewhere or other), likely to remain so.

Occasionally, sharp-eyed people thought Athene a bit too perfect and said (particularly women, and mothers of girls), "You can't somehow get *at* her," and "It doesn't seem natural to be all sunshine like that." But this was surprisingly rare.

It was also wrong.

All sunshine she was not, and her summery face was the very highest achievement, the head behind it holding dismal and complex troubles, the first though not the worst being her name. For though "Athene" is not perhaps such an unlikely name when taken down fast with Sebastian and Phoebe, it isn't a name people feel comfortable with—less comfortable then than now, for this was some years back when middle-class English females were called breezy, artless names that went well with tennis. "Athene" has very queer overtones, dazzling associations awakening larger-than-life memories of the illustrations in Charles Kingsley. "Athene," one remembers, had a most disagreeable birth, unconventional passions, and yet somehow or other was holy. It is even today a name uncommon among vicars' daughters.

Her friends called her Ath or Athie, her aunts Theeny; her brother, hence, called her Teeny-Theeny or Weeny-Theeny (she was tall) or Assie; her sister called her At and her mother called her Mim. Only her father called her Athene (he had chosen it; her mother had wanted Mildred) and then always after a few tries at something else, for by this time his great age had made one name much the same as another, and sometimes Athene turned out to be Agnes—his sister, dead in the Boer War—and sometimes Ivy. Nobody knew who Ivy had been.

Another trouble—a darker cloud—was the business of her father's age. She could remember no time when he had not been very old indeed. He had been seventy when she was born and from being about five years old she could remember particular kinds of smiles now and then when she was with him—especially in the post office, where they weren't really village people—odd looks at school on sports day, and a terrible ice cream on the promenade at Scarborough: "How about one for Grandpa too, then?" There was something astonishing here, unnatural, unthinkable. Hush!

After all, Beams was younger. He had been even older when Beams was born and you could see Beams never gave it a thought. Not a thought. There are thoughts that must never . . .

She was glad when she became too old to take his hand and feel his old fingers and want instead another hand between, tough and warm and jumping her along; and, guilty about this, she spent as much time with her father as possible, being charming, smiling, going walks with him. They were a usual sight in the holidays, walking about the woods or over onto the moors, tall and lively and talkative, both of them, their hair blown back, the Rector noble as Wordsworth. "That's a grand lass, that big one oft Rector's," they said round about. At school she wrote to him every week and only now and then to her mother. She seldom invited anybody home.

But in spite of wondering now and then about her name, her father knew Athene well. From the beginning she had announced her difficulties to him, arriving suddenly in his

11

study and putting her hand down across the page of his book so that he looked down at her. "I am going liquid," she had once said, at six. He had nodded in concern. He had been reading her *The Little Mermaid* and understood and remembered the reason why she hated the pattern of the chintz chair where her chin had been resting as the story got out of hand. "Stop," she had commanded.

"It'll be all right," he had said. "Hmmm, I'll just look at the end." Then he had shut the book and said, "No. You're quite right. We won't finish it. It's *not* very nice." But of course she had finished it later alone and remembered every line of the terrible drawing of the water that had been the mermaid spilling down to mix forever with the sea.

She had said outright to her father one day, "I wish I had a good straight name like Joan or something."

"Why?"

"Well. I don't know. Athene's a bit mad."

"There've been Joans mad, poor souls!"

"Or Emily."

"There've been Emilys maddish."

"Oh, no! No!" she had cried, so vigorously that he took off his gold glasses and stared.

For Athene's private madness—the really great distraction behind her quiet face—was a fairly odd one and to do with Emily Brontë.

It had started at school when they had been having *Jane Eyre* in sewing when she was nearly thirteen. Sewing was Wednesdays after tea, and very nice indeed except for the ones that liked games, which Athene did not, though she played them well enough and without grumbling. It was an old-fashioned school and they all sat around with bits of calico over their desks and the sewing on top, usually tablecloths or awful

12

blouses, and Miss Whatever-it-was read a book to them. The form room was pale green and after tea the low sun shone in through the trees outside and made it dapply. The book that was read was not meant to be work and you were never asked questions on it, so that there was no need to listen and you seldom did. Jane Eyre had been orphaned, cast out by her aunt, gone burning through Lowood Institution and deposited at Thornfield without Athene taking much account of her. "Novels," her mother used to say, "are a bit frivolous for Mim." Also, as someone said, the sewing mistress's voice sounded like marmalade.

Then—the chapter when Jane stood like a ghost in the road—the mistress was called away and handed the book to Athene as she left the room, and Athene, putting down the leg-o'-mutton sleeve, picked the book up, dropped it, opened it at the frontispiece and found herself looking at her own face.

At first she thought it must be some illustration of a scene in the book and was interested and pleased and thought she might start taking a bit more notice. She almost turned to the girl next to her and said, "I say, look! Isn't it like me?" but then she noticed that she was not alone on the page. There were some other women there—a tense-looking gathering with great black eyes and slightly sticking-out teeth as though they'd sucked their fingers too much as babies. She looked again at the one like herself with the biggest eyes and a great, long, marvelous neck. "My goodness!" She turned to the girl next to her. "Who's that like?" she asked. The others had all started talking. Someone said—a mousy person in the front row— "Are we going on with it, Athie?"

"Who's it like?" she asked.

"A dying duck in a thunderstorm," said the girl next to her.

"Go *on*," said the mouse. "It's nice."

Athene began to read about pale Jane under the moon, the galloping horse getting nearer and nearer, the ice, the fall, the hurt ankle, the dark, disagreeable man. When the bell went she sat on with the blouse on her knee, and missed supper and read on and on until someone came in and switched on the light and made her jump. "Ath—you're crazy. It's pitch dark. You *can't* have been reading." She went on through Prep and until the lights were put out in bed, and started again in the morning. At breakfast she read the preface and after lunch went to the library and found Mrs. Gaskell. She discovered that the long-necked girl was not Charlotte Brontë nor Jane Eyre, but Emily the sister, and got out Emily's poems and at the weekend bought *Wuthering Heights* from Smith's in the town because both school library copies were out. And she discovered that she had lived before.

"Which, if you come to think about it," she said to herself, carefully lighting a Bunsen burner and regarding it with concentration, "is insane. I don't know what I am talking about." ("Athie dear, your hair! For heaven's sake, tie it back!")

"I look like her, but no one could say . . . I mean, she was violent. Flinging those vicars out! Holding open those great iron gates and shouting!" (She had read *Shirley* now and knew that Shirley and Emily were one person.) "And being so difficult, and everyone being worried about whether she'd behave properly. 'Was Emily all right?'—Charlotte dashing out to ask someone if Emily had been unbearable on a walk on the moors. 'Emily never goes out with anyone.'

"I'm not like that. I am the absolute opposite. They call all over the place. They call, 'Athie, are you coming for a *walk? Where are* you?' I always say yes."

("Athie dear, the litmus paper!")

14

"And the wailing and crying round the house at night—her own self she thought it was, I'm sure. And all the firing of guns with the old father. I would never wail and cry in front of people, dead or alive. I have never wailed and cried in my life. And I really don't care at all for guns.

"And then—Heathcliff?"

She carefully measured drops into a test tube.

"But I know I do like her. I like her very much. And I do look like her. And the bread—being so good at making bread—that's me. And the moors. And the stone floors. The dovecote, the great long walks in the rain and the storms. I adore storms. There is just the wicket between our house and the churchyard, just like theirs—the wicket where the coffins went. . . ."

A sort of drooping look that had come over her disappeared. "Rubbish," she said. "Rubbish. We're not on the moors. Our house is lovely—all sun and open doors and big fires and cheerful, not like that miserable place. And Father's strong as a lion. (Though so was hers.)

"I do look like her, though. I do look like her. And I'm pretty clever, too."

"Athie! To see you over that test tube is giving me blood pressure. *Will* you concentrate! This is dangerous. It's not like you."

"Oh, goodness, sorry!"

"To look at you this moment no one would think you had a brain in your head."

Most of the class looked up and giggled.

"Sorry." Athene smiled quickly at the Chemistry mistress, who at once smiled back. (There was a university award here in three or four years.)

"You'd be sure," Athene thought, "you'd be sure all right I

15

had no brain if you knew. You'd drop dead if you knew what I was thinking this minute. If I said to you now—now—'Please, Miss Beecroft, I've just discovered that I am Emily Brontë.' Oh God, please help me. Please let me stop these thoughts."

"I've finished, Miss Beecroft," she said in a minute and passed up a page of clearly written figures.

"Oh, lovely," said Miss Beecroft. "Lovely work," she said, looking it through.

"Emily's handwriting was terrible. She couldn't write at all for years. At seventeen it was still atrocious. She was a poet. She was absolutely different from me. She wouldn't have had a word to say to me."

("What is the matter with Athene Price? Is she in love or something? Fourteen? No.")

"Yet I know I am her. I know I am her. I never utter. I smile and smile. I am a dreary great hopeless dove. That's what I am. Everyone would say so. But I know I am her."

("Whatever will happen when that one does fall in love!")

Doing a quadratic equation a few days later, easily, steadily working it out, her head decoratively, gravely bent, her parting straight, her fingernails clean, Athene suddenly thought, "My God! I am possessed. I am insane," and blushed scarlet.

Chapter Three

My dear Sybil,

I have thought of you so much since last Friday and wished that I had spent more time with you, but I know you so well that I have no fears at all that you will not understand. People like darling Posie are a bit of a trial on these occasions and I had to give her a lot of attention. I had been worried all the morning about the egg sandwiches, with P. coming. As you saw I am sure, there were not enough. Boo of course had wanted them *thicker*—I suppose to put people off. But Posie was always like a dog (remember school) and there's never enough. Boo of course is not domesticated. Matrons of schools have everything done for them and grow childish, though I suppose one shouldn't speak ill of one's sister to someone outside the family.

But you, dear Syb, I have never thought of as outside the

family and you know of course that Alfred thought the same. In fact he asked me particularly before he died—oh quite some time ago—to be sure to see that you had something of his as a little memento. I am sending you therefore the crucifix we brought back with us from Perugia in 1928—our honeymoon —and which he always—[Here Mrs. Price paused, having a strict regard for what passes for truth.]—kept in a drawer. It is a little broken but the figure is good don't you think? I hope you don't mind soapstone. It will be difficult to think of a way of getting it to you economically but I expect I shall master this little problem as I have learned to master so many.

As you know—or perhaps you don't. Few people do—we have to leave the Rectory within six weeks of Alfred's death. It is Law. I shall be very busy packing up and really more than busy—sick, dear Syb, and somewhat in the hands of Our Lord as to where we shall go. We have always been, as you know, very poor and shall now be in ABSOLUTE PENURY. Men of Alfred's genius are like this about money. Of course it is a great test of our Faith and I am intending simply to await Direction and let the Lord provide.

Now—the school holidays start next week and the week after and I don't want the children about me just now. I must seem odd, but you who knew the full wonder of Alfred will understand. Therefore, dear, may Athene come and stay with you, say July 26th, for two weeks, arriving 12.25 from Appleby. I mean deps. Appleby 12.25 (school train, seen off by Seb who is going to rendezvous with her there—or perhaps York?—M'bro 2.25—on his way to Scotland) arrives M'bro 3.37. If she gets bus on to Cook's Cove. arrives 5.20. If you meet her M'bro it is Platform 1. I will send her holiday clothes on to you in a large parcel (registered) probably tomorrow or the day after. She is a dear girl and so fond of you and although

18

I know she would want to be with me at this time, I am sure it would be better for her not to come home. A second unhappy—[she looked at her watch]—homecoming would be depressing, even though she is SO STEADY—just like her father. Sebby and Phoebe are nicely fixed up or of course I would have sent you more of us. People are *so very good*.

Bless you, Syb, and we shall have a good talk soon. How quickly our lives pass. I cannot imagine how anyone can SURVIVE without a faith in God. By the way Mim can bring the crucifix with her. I shall take it to Seb when I get him off after school and he can give it to her at Appleby (or York). *Don't thank me*, dear. It was Alfred's wish.

Ever loving Dodo.

P.S. Forgot to say going back Mim could get 2.23 from M'bro to (I think) Keighley where there's a connection to Ilkley where Posie goes, or perhaps to Preston if Posie is at Southport (Plat 5) (August 15). But I will write again. If it is Preston, will you remind her to get

> 1 half-pound Cheddar
> 1 half-pound double Gloucester
> $\frac{1}{4}$ lb. Wensleydale

from that marvelous shop at the top of the street near the market. I have saved cheese coupons—we don't care for cheese—and food is really all you can send Posie as you know. A crucifix would be quite wasted.

The *salt* cheddar with the rind.

Newton Abbey, Friday

My darling old Posie,
It was really lovely to see you at the funeral and looking so

19

well. It was good of you to say how much you enjoyed the tea. This is our Faith, dear. Life must go on.

What a way for you to come! I hope your chauffeur was not exhausted and you got the dinner you had planned in York.

Well, it was a sad day and yet illumined with brightness I shall not forget nor confuse with my sorrow. To see so many old friends again was a great comfort. The children as you saw were very calm. Mim of course is never anything else, bless her. Didn't you think Sebastian looked splendid?

Now, about Athene—your offer to do something I am going to accept without a qualm, Posie, and if it is convenient to you she will be arriving on the 2.25 at Scarborough on the 15th (August) and could stay with you for a week or two. Then could you get her on a train to Sybil Bowles at Cook's Cove? She is a Dismal Desmond—and not well. That leg looks worse to me, though Alfred always said that it was nervous—but after all that Alfred did for her spiritually I don't see why she should not give a little hospitality back. He has left her really quite a *large* present. I had as a matter of fact hoped that darling M might have gone to her first, but I have had no answer to my two letters and when one rings up they always say she is lying down. So I shall have to send details later of how long she will be with you, and will send off her holiday clothes to you in a large parcel (registered) tomorrow or the day after. You, as a Clergy Daughter, know that we have to be out of here in six weeks—after 16 years! More—Mim was born here and she is seventeen in September. But we are all tenants *everywhere*. I was hoping to send you some cheese from Preston but this seems unlikely now with Sybil muddling it. I expect it is her age—and the leg.

I will write more fully of course later,

Your loving Dodo.

20

P.S. Athene is a superb cook if yours should be on holiday. I will send you some jam. I can hardly transport it all to whatever boarding house we shall no doubt move to. I am thinking of the South.

D.

Newton Abbey, Monday

Dear Boo,

I've been trying to get Mim fixed up—the others are settled. Seb is going to this curious Buddhist place in Scotland, though I don't know how they got there—so cold after India—and Beams is off to those nice sailing people in Wales. Mim refuses point-blank (unlike her) to go to any school friends, so I've fixed up I hope with that dreary Sybil Bowles and poor old Posie. At least she will be fed and quiet and comfortable if not exactly inspired. Anyhow, I know that Alfred would not approve of all this South of France nonsense—skiing etc.— even if we had the chance of it. I suppose there is no skiing in August anyway!

Here Mrs. Price stopped and gazed about the huge, empty drawing room for a while. A lot of furniture had gone into store and the sun shone on the parquet floor she had had put in by the Church Commissioners and on which she had always hoped to give dances.

"We are to be out by the 14th," she wrote. She stopped again and this time looked for a long time straight in front of her. Unpruned roses tapped the long windows. The fine gravel was growing a green haze.

"I have various plans," she wrote. "One is a curate in need of a housekeeper." She stopped again, and then attacked the paper with her usual vigor.

"Thank you for your help at the funeral, Boo. I'm sorry about the egg sandwiches. By the way, did you see Alfred's binoculars anywhere? I believe he did say once that you were to have them, but it may be necessary to sell absolutely everything, just to keep body with soul. I have just been telling old Posie how badly off we are. Dear Posie, she hasn't the slightest idea how rich she is. How lovely not to *have* to know, or to have a splendid regular salary like you.

"I shall write to you about trains. I shall have to write to everybody about trains again as I see that I have been consulting *winter* timetables. When you meet Mim (Did I ask this before? Could you have Mim for a while when she comes over from Sybil's about September 10th? It will be *around* September 10th. After your Red Cross do of course) will you keep her for a bit and then drive her to Darlington MID SEPTEMBER to meet up with Seb who will be coming over from the Buddhists—he hasn't given me the exact date. It may be earlier—and they can travel south together (if I do fix on Putney). I'll send our rope ladder with her. You might like it for your juniors. I shan't leave it here for the next man. If they appoint who I think they'll appoint he is practically a *Roman*. Love, Do."

In the end it was York. Sebastian with a great pack on his back and very short hair looked up at Athene's carriage window.

"Have a good time," he said.

"Same to you."

Parcels were being thrown about round the guard's van.

"Do you *like* Buddhism?"

"Oh, well . . ."

"Do you know where she is?"

22

"No—she's going to write."

"She does nothing else but write."

"Do you know where you're going?" he asked, smiling. A whistle blew.

"Not really. I don't think I do."

"Where's the jam?"

They smiled at each other and the train began to move.

"Write," she cried suddenly. His face had become stony.

"Well, it may be difficult."

"Do write." She felt her own face begin to twitch about. "Beams never does."

"Writing her memoirs."

"Only to herself," she said, trying to smile. He turned away with a wave and swung round under the great rucksack, looking at the ground. She sat back in the carriage, adjusted the jam, pushed one of her suitcases along the floor with her foot. In her handbag was a wad of letters and instructions. She would get them out soon. She supposed she did know where she was going. She must have bought a ticket not ten minutes ago. But all was blank. She watched hygienic York slide away, the white Minster, the green sewage ponds. "I really don't know where I'm going," she informed the flat colorless fields. "Nor do I much care."

Chapter Four

It was Posie's and Ilkley. Posie's was not really Ilkley, for she lived in Scarborough, but Posie was on her summer holidays and the Scarborough house under dust sheets with empty flower vases and the leathery old maid eating dripping toast with the papers at all hours of the day and not always in her own quarters.

Posie was often away from home, every autumn at Southport for the dahlias, every summer at northern spas, of which Ilkley—although people said the war had finished it and you scarcely saw a hat—was still her favorite, with amazingly good cake shops, doctors, healing springs and a distinguished hydropathic hotel called Crag Foot just outside the town. "Crag Foot!" she used to say contentedly each June as her gray Daimler turned into the curving drive—a rather shabby drive after the fashion of the best stately homes. "Oh, how lovely that the war is over."

Crag Foot was tall and gray, hideous and immensely

expensive. Old pale pink tennis courts stood on one side of it, cracked like the surface of the moon, and leather jungles of laurel and rhododendron trailed off on the other. A winding stone wall enclosed the lot, and beyond the stone wall spread the moors. The wild, heathery wind blew on all sides, beating at the Victorian window frames with a noise that gave the illusion of health without ever approaching the complexion. Long, quiet corridors concealed throughout the year some hundred or so soft-skinned, elderly people who could all come down to dinner in a different outfit for evenings on end. Dozens and dozens of diamond engagement rings gleamed nightly for an hour over after-dinner cards.

In the summer, well-heeled families sometimes appeared for a week and used Crag Foot as a family hotel, and sometimes the heads of old-fashioned businesses—mackintoshes and shoes—were to be found there in twos and threes ("You'll meet them all," said Beams, "Freeman, Hardy *and* Willis!"). But mostly it was old ladies.

But at Ilkley station Athene was met only by a car, as it was Posie's Treatment Hour. Posie in the foyer of Crag Foot was standing under a potted palm, rather flustered. She would *never* have *chosen* to let Athene arrive like this, she said, never, never, never. She hugged her and nodded and smiled and hugged her again. She hardly reached Athene's shoulder and seemed without a bone in her body. It had always been so. Athene's earliest memories had always held Auntie Posie, fat and soft and well and happy, smiling at her: Auntie Posie on the garden steps, Auntie Posie eating strawberries in the basket chair, Auntie Posie at the pantomime at York joining in all the choruses, shining with love. Always Auntie Posie's birthday present arriving first, always her Christmas present the biggest and the best.

Lovely pearls rose and fell contentedly now above Posie's modesty vest and brown wool cardigan suit. She wore no diamond engagement ring—her father (a rich bishop) had always been everything to her and had been a long time dying, releasing her rather past marriageable age.

"Oh, Athie!" she cried, "oh dear, oh dear!" and the familiar feel of the cardigan brought surprising comfort.

There was tea in a long room with sofas and round tables. Ladies whispered in small groups. Occasionally as they passed down the room someone acknowledged Posie with a quick nod and quicker, polite glance at Athene, but Posie waddled steadfastly ahead to her own sofa, where at once a waiter slid up and settled cushions. "We have tea here every day," she said, "at a quarter to four. Dinner is at seven and they like you to be rather punctual, dear. Then we come in here for coffee and a little chat and canasta and cards. We have morning coffee in here, too, unless we take the car into Ilkley—they have nice coffee in Lucy's—and lunch is at one. Do you like morning tea, dear? You can have it from seven, and breakfast is at nine and always three courses."

"How lovely," Athene said.

"Have an asparagus sandwich. These toasted buns are very nice."

"They're gorgeous," said Athene. There was a pause that seemed to get rather long.

"I hope it's all right for me to be here," Athene said at last. She remembered that Posie had not actually written to her about the visit—all instructions had been in her mother's letters.

"It's lovely, dear."

"I mean—I do hope Mother didn't, well, ask." The pause recurred. Athene found herself thinking that in all the

26

years—the panto, the ballet, the picnics, the Scarborough Open Air *Hiawatha*—she had never been alone with Posie.

"It's lovely to have you, dear."

She had a watery, distant look. Had she always had that look? Was it how she showed being in a huff? Oh, *no!* Perhaps she had dropsy. She was awfully fat. An awful vision came of Posie suddenly . . . Athene gulped and said breathlessly, "Are you quite well these days, Auntie?"

"Oh, yes, dear."

"Er—Mother is quite well. She sends her love." (Funny how she never asked questions. What was it Father said about people who never ask you anything?)

"Oh, good, dear."

"She's very busy, of course, getting—er—"

"Have another scone. Let's ask for more jam."

"Oh, no, thanks. Unless you—"

"Yes, I think so. Jack, more jam, please. Shall we have two dishes more, do you think?"

"Er—"

Posie munched on, smiling, and when she met Athene's eyes after the arrival of the jam, gave additional little smiles and nods and said, "Strawberry and black-currant jelly." The quiet room grew quieter, with only an occasional clink or murmur. "It's like one of those ghastly novels where nothing ever happens," Athene thought. "Ghastly Virginia Woolf or Proust."

"What do we—you—do after tea as a rule?" she asked.

"Well, I usually have a little rest, dear. I expect you would like a little rest."

"Oh, no—I'm not a bit tired."

"I expect you *will* be tired, dear. We all get very tired here. It's the air. We always find that new people seem to get tired.

27

It's quite funny to hear them, anybody new. After just a little while they say, 'D'you know, Posie, I'm *quite tired.*' "

"Oh, I'm sure I shan't be—"

"It's the wind, I think. It's so noisy, dear. You'll have trouble getting used to the wind. It's right off the moors. It can be quite frightening, especially at night. But I'm never frightened of anything really. I'm very lucky." She laughed and munched.

"Oh, I love the wind—"

"Well, it's very healthy, dear. Now, can you just help—yes, thank you, dear, that's right. Shall we go up? They've got lovely lifts, you know."

Together they trudged toward a large cage with golden traceries, filled with mahogany and mirrors.

"There is ping-pong, of course," said Posie. "If you'd rather find the ping-pong—"

They tramped back down the lounge again and through some baize doors to a ballroom. It was in darkness and they fumbled for lights. A ping-pong table was revealed at the far end of it with the net limp and no sign of bats. Dust hung thick in the folds of the stage curtain behind it. "Oh, dear, no one about," said Posie. "I believe there is to be a dance, though, soon."

Back they went and into the lift. Very, very slowly and with a slight swing they rose upward, very, very slowly they began to walk down the silent, wide corridor toward the window at the end with its blind half drawn down, the acorn string just not touching the big polished plant below it in its spinach-green pot.

"You'll be quite quiet. Have a nice sleep. Your room is two hundred—yes, here we are. I have the key. Quite near mine." A pale, soft hand on a brass door handle, a mountainous soft

28

bed, a writing desk, a dead, oval mirror. All cream, all dustless, all still. The shocking, astounding vision came again: Posie in bed with no clothes on, lying there eating jam. Putting her paw in like a bear. And oh! The face her own!

"AUNTIE POSIE!" It came out a shriek. It astonished them both. Like a cry of Fire. "Auntie Posie, do you think I might just go out? Just—actually, just for a little? It's the train—fresh air. To get a little air? Would you mind?"

"Of *course*." The kind eyes looked up. "Of course, dearie—"

"I'll go by the stairs. Yes. Yes, please. Yes, Auntie. It's all right. No, I don't need a coat. Look, I'll just drop it here, could I, please?" It fell at the feet of the green pot. "Goodbye. Thank you very much. I'm just off. Don't worry." She began to walk fast, at the stairhead to run. Down she ran, down she flew, stair rods flashing, hurtling past a motionless maid—white cap and tray—out into the main hall, out of the wide doors, anywhere, anywhere ("Athene is so calm"). Left? Right? Into the laurels and down the rhododendron path, puffing and blowing, hair flying. "I shall die. It is limbo. I am dead already. I must go. I can't stay here. I can't."

But she stopped. The path stopped. It stopped before a rustic summerhouse deep in gloom. It had begun to rain in big, heavy drops and the noise of the rain on the thick leaves rattled angrily all round her.

It was a dismal noise, a dismal place, but she didn't notice. For on the summerhouse steps stood Heathcliff.

29

Chapter Five

He said nothing, but continued to stand watching her, leaning against the tree-trunk door frame, smoking a cigarette. His eyes were heavy and sleepy, his hair very thick and long, his mouth discontented, rather curly, clear-cut.

The rain became a torrent. Enormous thunder drops, icy cold, fell on her bare arms and there was an actual clap of thunder and a blast of wind. He didn't move out of the way for her or even sideways to let her get past him into the summerhouse, but waited and watched her.

There wasn't room to rush past. She must, of course. She must say, "Oh, please, mind? Can I come in? I'm soaked," and she tried. But she had been running so hard she found she couldn't speak at all. She stood in rivers of rain, her chest going up and down, and not able to stop looking at him.

Then there was the most tremendous clap of thunder and she ran at him straight, fell into the summerhouse, pushing him out of the way. "Oh, heavens," she said with her back to him, and heard her voice go what Beams called boarding-school. Her head was bent. She shook water out of her hair with her back to him. "I'm so *wet*," and she turned round, widening her eyes with the smile she used on admiring Upper Thirds, making them swoon.

But he had gone.

"I say," she called.

She looked all round the summerhouse, then put her head outside. She even stepped out into the rain again and looked about.

He was not there. The avenue she had run down was empty. Curtains of rain blew across it, rhododendrons tossed.

"I say," she called, "where've you gone? You'll get soaked. Come back.

"Do come back," she called more plaintively. He must be somewhere. No ghost had such a face.

She started trying to dry off her hair on her handkerchief and her arms on her skirt. She shook herself and went to the door again. The rain had settled down to a steady onslaught. The thunder and wind seemed to have stopped. "I'm a fool," she thought. "Good heavens, what a fool!" But she felt happy. She started laughing, put down her head, covered her ears up with her hands and plunged back down the path and into the hotel. "So *wet!*" she cried, dazzling the porter. Wrapping herself up in thick pink towels, she paraded about her bathroom in clouds of thundering steam. She arranged another towel about her head, looked in the glass and let her mouth hang open. "Miss Vermeer," she said, then made herself stern and noble: "The Doge of Venice."

Steam obscured all. Dropping the towels, she stepped into the bath, bowing to left and right, and in a deep voice said hello to the taps. "They'd never know me," she thought.

31

"That's a real nice girl of Miss Dixon's," said one waitress to another at dinner, and Posie said, "You've got some color in your cheeks."

And all that evening she felt splendid, through dinner and coffee and canasta with Posie and her friend Mrs. Messenger. She felt splendid at bedtime, sinking into the wonderful bed, so different from school, so different from home with all its familiar knobs and valleys. The bedside light had an expensive satisfying click as you switched it off. She felt her face smiling as she fell asleep. She kept seeing him as thoughts blurred and changed into dreams, and, leaping at her suddenly, she saw also her father's face, quizzical and wry. "Joy cometh in the morning," it said. It woke her up completely, for she had thought that she couldn't remember it. That face had quite vanished since the day they sent for her at school, and she sat up in the expensive bed, looking in front of her for a long time.

In the morning she felt happy still and gazed with love at the chambermaid drawing back her curtains, with love at the silver toast rack and flowers on the breakfast table and outside the window at the brilliant sun. "Too bright," said Mrs. Messenger, plodding past. "There'll be thunder again before bedtime."

From Posie's table you could just see the moors. You looked across lawns to the wall, and there was a small purple horizon. The wind battered and banged.

"This is a lovely place, Auntie Posie."

"I'm going to have kidneys," said Posie.

"The moors look quite near."

"Oh, they are, dear. It's not far from the Brontë country, you know."

32

Quickly, as she followed Posie out, she looked all round the room: but he was not there.

She felt good, though, still, getting ready to go into Ilkley in the big, quiet car with Posie and Mrs. Messenger sitting with their knees a bit spread, side by side, with their library books in string bags. In the library she wandered away from them and turned the corner of every bookcase with a sort of eager, pleasant feeling. I'm on a thread, she thought, and smiled very brightly at the young man behind the counter. Then in Lucy's, over a cream cake, she became aware that he was sitting at the table behind her and at last looked as they got up to go. But he had disguised himself as an ex-colonel with scarlet face and watery blue eye.

Under the hanging baskets they walked, pausing at antique shops. Mrs. Messenger bought a reel of green embroidery silk. There was great discussion about the green. She hadn't brought the pattern with her. Now, if it should turn out that this reel were a little *light*, might she be allowed to come back and change it for one a *trifle* darker? They were fourpence-halfpenny. Such a price! Otherwise, of course, she would have considered buying the two. This green was a *risk*. Oh, how kind.

Athene's stomach turned over as they reached the car and a dark man went by smelling of nice tobacco. But he was ancient. Touching thirty. And a knitted tie.

At the hotel steps a glance through the rhododendrons revealed nothing, nor did the lounge for sherry, nor the dining room for lunch, nor the foyer coming out. She looked at everyone. The waiters were all old, the porters very much like porters.

"I have a little rest now," said Posie. "Then my Treatment

Hour. Then tea. Shall we meet at tea, dear? Can you amuse yourself till then?"

"Oh, yes, that's fine. Yes, I'm quite all right."

"Then I'll go up. Don't get too tired. Perhaps you'll find someone to play tennis with. Or there may be somebody on the courts to watch. They don't get used much, though, I'm afraid!

"You aren't bored, dear?" she said in the lift through the bars.

"No—no. Of course not."

The fat, anxious face ascended.

She went out onto the steps, then came back and took a newspaper and set off again into the hot afternoon. Another quick look at the rhododendron path—but she felt annoyed with it and turned her back and went walking round the other way over a croquet lawn and down into a long, secluded avenue with herbaceous plants towering on each side. A long wooden seat with curling metal arms was standing on the path between, the white paint flaking a little. She leaned back. Above the delphiniums was a minute purple triangle of moors. It was very quiet except for bees. Red-hot pokers, tiger lilies blazed and there was the heavy smell of catmint and lavender. Closing her eyes, she thought, "In a moment I will hear his feet upon the path."

There wasn't a sound.

"Oh, what has happened to me?" she thought. Later she got up and walked on, turning away from the flower garden to the tennis courts. She could see their high wire-netting sides in front of her, and, trailing her fingers in them, walked all round their edges to the pavilion. The nets sagged. Nobody played.

But she noticed two tennis rackets lying on the far court,

34

two or three tennis balls lying about and a blue denim jacket pushed through the wire netting, and she stopped for a moment. The sun beat down. They might have been there a hundred years.

She walked over to the pavilion, which had its windows shuttered up and an old basket chair turning to straw on its veranda and a hapless sort of cushion. She paused, sighed and went up to it, tapping the *Daily Telegraph* along the veranda railings; and with a violent scuffling noise within, someone leaped across the pavilion floor and slammed the door.

It was the boy, and not only the boy but someone else, and not only someone else but something else. As Beams never stopped saying, nobody understands eyes and what they see and how fast. In the blink of the door's slamming she had seen something most peculiar and dreadful. She had seen the soles of two feet, crossed over each other and belonging to someone lying on something disturbingly low. They were yellowish feet, with lines on them. And they were definitely female.

She fled like a thief over the grass, round the courts and away through the red-hot pokers, only calming down to go more steadily at the croquet lawn, which faced a battery of windows. She passed under them at last and into the airless drive, where beside an arc of petunias Mrs. Messenger stood, heavily examining the reel of cotton.

Mrs. Messenger said, "Aha, then. There you are. Don't despair. Oh yes, I saw you despair. I can see that much. I'm not your aunt. What have you been up to?"

"I think I must—"

"Been scouting about? That's right. Seeing what's on offer? Come along, we'll sit down. I was expecting the car but . . . Here. The bench under the trees. I expect you're very bored."

35

"No—oh, no."

"Well, you ought to be bored if you're not. I can't think this is much of a holiday for you. Where's your mother?"

"Oh, she's—well, she's moving us."

"Not helping her?"

"She won't let me. Any of us."

"Yes. I've met her. Selling up, isn't she?"

"Well—actually, Mrs. Messenger, I think I'll go in. I've got a bit of a headache."

"Too bright. I said so this morning. The day's too bright. When do you go?"

"Well, I think I'll go now if you—"

"No. When do you leave Posie?"

"Oh—two weeks. I think it's to be two or three weeks."

"And then?"

"I'm going to another friend of Mother's."

"Maybe there'll be someone for you there."

"I'm—I'm sorry?"

Mrs. Messenger leaned over and put a fat pink hand with short fingers on Athene's knee. "It's a nice boy you want."

"Excuse—"

"Posie's mad, poor duck. D'you know the story? Father wanted a son. Mother died. Father furious."

"Mrs.—"

"Fathers! Mind, *your* father was good to her. She managed. Very rich, of course, but she manages the money now, all right. People batten."

"Oh—"

Mrs. Messenger's eyes were closely examining the cotton reel. "They get a lot out of her, you know. Free this and that. Not cheap, living here half the year. *I* know that."

36

"She's very kind." Athene was scarlet. "She's sweet, Auntie Posie. She's awfully fond of us."

"Oh, yes. Yes, we all know *that*. Mos *tawfully*"—Mrs. Messenger was a coarse woman—"fond. Godmother, I suppose?"

"She's—she's Sebastian's. My brother's."

"I suppose he'll get the emeralds."

"I'm terribly sorry. I must go in. I've got a head—"

"Not the pearls, I dare say. You'll get the pearls. Very nice for you, too. They'll suit you. It doesn't seem fair, though. Some people have all . . . I suppose you know she's got funny habits?"

But Athene was running away.

Chapter Six

The letter was waiting for her at the reception desk. The porter called to her as she flew by.

My Lamb,

Here I am in Larpent Avenue but the curate is quite unsuitable and I'm not at all sure of *Putney*. There are streets and streets of the ugliest houses I have ever seen in my life with nasty coarse gardens full of dahlias and sunflowers. Church all right but smells damp and the notices on the boards positively *spotted* with age. Low, I should say. Two candles and one of those dreadful lecterns. There is simply no one here we know and they seem hardly to have heard of Yorkshire. I have other strings to my bow and will write again from Richmond. (There is a Richmond down here with quite a nice view, like ours, but duller. There is a park, etc.)

I should really prefer to be right in the middle of London where the people are less south-country, and I knew the

Bishop of Pimlico's wife once—Aggie Deans. Her mother was nothing at all (white *cotton* gloves) but she gets things done and she has absolutely *made* that husband. Writes his sermons, so they say. I am in touch with her though she has not yet answered. I expect the reason is that black doll of yours her awful Priscilla broke when you were three. You were such a saint—you never said *one word*. Not a tear. They never replaced it nor even said they were sorry, or not adequately. But it is a pity I dropped her so thoroughly.

Darling—how are you getting on with Posie? Absolutely nothing will happen there, but I think that this is just what you want—and with Sybil and Boo. A long quiet time. Now I must write to Seb and Phoebe. Don't reply here. I shall be gone. I will write from the next place which might just possibly be the Isle of Wight.

My darling Mim, say your prayers, not particularly for us for we have nothing to fear (see Matthew vi.28: lilies of field) but for the poor people of Putney who are entirely without occupation other than stirring their tea about. The streets round Larpent Avenue are utterly silent and everyone makes a great point of not knowing the people next door. A curious Christianity and I have told both them and this curate and continue to do so. They have not one word to say in reply.

Your ever loving Mother.

"Now, givers," as Beams once said ominously, "are worth watching."

"Worth knowing," said Sebastian. "What's the matter? Has someone given you a bomb?"

"Worth watching," said Beams. "Giving isn't necessarily all right."

"What rubbish is this?" asked their mother, passing by and

out of sight toward the post office. "We are told that it is more blessed to give than—"

"More attractive," said Beams, "that's all. And only then until you look at motives."

"No motive—almost no motive can be as bad as being mean," said Seb. "Being that sort I really hate. You, for instance. You never give anyone anything. Nor does Athene, come to that."

"I do give things when I like people," said Beams. "I can't help liking people so seldom."

"Athene likes everybody and never gives a thing."

"That," said Beams, "is only because it never occurs to her. You can't blame her for that. If you ask, she'll give you anything she's got. Make you a dress or a cake. She doesn't think by herself, that's all. Just broods.

"Father, of course," she went on, "gives things all over the place. If money falls out of his pocket, he leaves it lying, thinking that the next one along might like it."

"Well, I agree there's nothing so wonderful about that."

"I admit pleasant," said Beams.

"Mother gives," said Seb.

"Oh, Mother gives, all right," said Beams with a dark look. "That's what I'm talking about."

But Beams was unfair. Mrs. Price was a giver and a real giver. She may only have given things she didn't want, or boomerangs that landed back nice and heavy on her own mat, or letters all about herself which left her feeling efficient and kind and their recipients reeling—but giving of any kind takes money and time and gum and string and fussy, crackling, brown paper and standing about at the post office. And letters—any letters, even completely self-centered ones—are better than no letters and a dead breakfast. Mrs. Price's letters in their way enlivened life, begat other letters and would be of some sort of interest to historians if anyone ever kept them. (Posie did.)

Moreover if you write as many letters as Mrs. Price, even if they take absolutely no thought whatsoever for other people's crucial moments, in a lifetime one or two stand a chance of arriving opportunely. Athene read, for instance, this one and, leaning against the back of her bedroom door, let it fall to the ground. Outside, the humiliating Mrs. Messenger still waited for a car to the needlework shop, the hall porter had not finished sorting the afternoon post, hardly five minutes had passed; yet Athene had recovered.

She sighed, straightened herself up, walked across the room, skirted the bed and the pillow she had been aiming for and sat down at the writing desk. As Beams said, she was no giver—beautiful people seldom are—but could give, having received, and her mother's letter, like a dotty governess, set her off. She answered it.

Then she wrote to her brother, her sister, her Chemistry mistress and a couple of girls at school. Her writing was small and round and black and went across the page in beautiful straight lines. She reread and folded each letter, putting them in a neat pile, addressing the ones she could address and sticking stamps on from her pocketbook, very straight. She got up, took off her skirt and blouse, washed her face, combed her hair, cleaned her nails. She put on an apple-green cotton dress with fourteen small white buttons down the front, beautifully made by herself. She looked at herself and walked back to the desk. The window it faced looked out at the croquet lawn and the back of the bright herbaceous border. The croquet hoops had shadows. It must be teatime.

Yes, it was. Ten past. They like you to be rather punctual.

How impeccable she felt, tall and graceful inside her nice clean dress. How still and calm she looked. How pure.

She sat down and in enormous, crooked letters wrote,

My darling,

Oh my darling. I love you, I adore you. I want you. My darling my darling my darling my darling my darling my darling my darling my darling. Always——Athene.

Excited and horrified, she tore this to bits and went down to the lounge.

And all the evening—there was some sort of a dance and she sat on a red plush tip-up seat between Posie and Mrs. Messenger and did a fox-trot with an old gentleman and a quick-step with an army officer with a long, clean chin—all the evening she thought about it. People danced about in front of her like shadows to and fro. "Who was I writing to?" she thought. Someone jigged and jigged before her, holding a red person with yellow hair, but she looked away from them, from one side to the other, dazed and almost blind. She kept thinking, "It's all over. It never happened. It won't happen now."

PART TWO

The End of August

Chapter Seven

Sybil Bowles drooped beside the bus stop under an umbrella outlined against a dismal sky. The bus stop at first appeared to be on the brink of a cliff, the road swinging up to it, then lurching away into an asphalt patch where the buses turned and went off back again to Carlinhow and Skinninggrove and Grinkle and similar obscurities. Cook's Cove was the end of the run.

When the brink and Sybil were approached, however, they were seen to be only at the beginning of a series of brinks which dropped lumpily downward with a stony, wide path between them, corkscrewing out of sight between brambles. The village was built—stuck—onto the cliff face so that you sat in your deckchair-sized garden looking down the chimneys of the people below.

Curving round the bay at the bottom of the cliff was a midget stretch of sea front with boats drawn up on it. There was a roundabout, parceled up in sacks and string, a barricaded ice-cream hut, dead as January. Not a soul in sight. The sea soaked inward into the brown cliffs across the bay, making some froth now and then. Sybil, Athene and the jumbled cottages regarded it all: high summer, cold, windless, the rain very fine and steady, as silent as the sea below and seemingly as permanent.

Sybil had sneezed when Athene got out of the bus. Beneath her bucket hat she seemed not to be at rest. Her white riding mac, tightly belted in, made her look thinner than ever, and when she turned sideways she might have been hanging up in a cupboard. (Emily Brontë's coffin was fifteen inches wide. Hush.) Her galoshes fluted upward like bats. With sinking heart Athene noticed that one leg was tightly bandaged under a serviceable stocking.

"Let me help with those," said Sybil, bending to Athene's suitcases and immediately dropping them both in the road. "Oh, dear, I'm so sorry, I'm not meant to lift."

"Heavens, I can carry them," Athene said. "Of course you can't. They're a bit heavy because of the crucifix and the rope ladder. Of course you mustn't. I've bought you some flowers."

Sybil received the bright Ilkley sweet peas gravely, gravely sniffed them and sneezed again.

"I thought we'd have some tea at the hotel. Oh, dear—isn't it wet? It's just here at the top of the cliff. It's been raining ever since we arrived. I expect it was the same at Ilkley?"

"No, it was very hot in Ilkley, actually. Terribly hot. Just a bit thundery. All the time."

Sybil looked sorrowfully round the empty hotel lounge and sank onto a low chair, easing her leg before her. They gazed round the room—tubular tables, old orange hessian curtains, paintings by the local artist, metal chairs that had once seemed daring, like the long, curved, rusting metal window frames

46

filled with colorless sky. "It rains a lot here," said Sybil. "I believe it is the wettest place on the northeast coast."

"I'm sure it's very—er—beautiful, though," said Athene.

"No, it isn't. No, it isn't beautiful," said Sybil. "If you want to know, it isn't beautiful at all," and she began to cry.

"Oh, dear." Athene jumped up and then sat down again as Miss Bowles began violently shaking her head. "Oh, goodness, Miss Bowles, I'm sorry. Is something wrong? Can I get you—"

A waitress approached and stood looking at them. She folded her arms and began feeling round her teeth with her tongue.

"Oh, please," said Athene.

"Now then," said the waitress.

"Please," said Athene, "my—er—friend isn't very well. Perhaps—could we have tea?"

"Aye," said the waitress, "I'll bring you some tea. Miss Bowles," she yelled suddenly, "Miss Bowles, love, be quiet now. Tek hold. I'll bring you yer tea directly."

"Not beautiful at all," sobbed Sybil.

"Certainly not if you carry on that way. Not fit to be seen, you're not. You stopping with them?"

"I'm just— I'm staying a while with—"

"Then God 'elp yer."

She departed and as Miss Bowles sniffed on and Athene faced her in silence, the processes of tea-making could be heard offstage—a quantity of water drumming into a heavy-sounding kettle, the chink of cups, the chopping up of rather hard butter. It wouldn't be quick. "It's Miss Bowles," they heard the waitress say, and a mumbling came from a distant pantry.

"I said 'Miss Bowles.' She's upset again. There's a young lass with her."

47

Mumble mumble.

"I said 'a young lass.' No, not *her*."

Mumble mumble.

"Aye, that's what I just said. 'God 'elp yer,' I said."

Mumble.

" 'GOD 'ELP YER,' " roared the waitress, and Miss Bowles went off again.

"Oh, please." Athene got up and went round. "Oh, please, Miss Bowles, what is it? What's the matter?"

"It's Primrose," she wept. "Oh, heavens, how could I? I ought to have said don't come. I did try to tell your mother it wouldn't do, but somehow I never can tell your mother things when she's got her own plans."

"Yes," Athene said, "I know what you mean."

"Your father, now," and she began to sob again.

"Miss Bowles. Look, Miss Bowles. Do hush a minute. I was just thinking. Shall I go? Honestly, I don't mind. I can go to Auntie Boo. I'm going there anyway the beginning of next week for her to run me to—somewhere or other to meet up with Seb. There's heaps of room—it's Seb's school. I've been before. She's the Matron. I really don't mind a bit if there's someone I'll upset."

"It's not that it's you, Theeny. You don't think I mean it's you. It's just that Primrose—"

"Er—who's Primrose?"

"She's Prim. Primmy. Primrose Clarke. Don't you know her?"

"No—I don't think—"

"I've always had holidays with Prim. She's English."

"English?"

"Yes."

"But, aren't you—"

48

"No, I'm Geography."

"Oh, yes, I see."

"We met at college." She wept again.

"Miss Bowles, oh, goodness, do hush. Look, here's tea."

A great tray bearing a metal teapot and milk jug and serviceable cups approached with the waitress behind it. There was a mountain of bread and butter cut in big triangles. "Now then," she said. "There now, soon have yer set up." She marched out.

"Of course she's a Housemistress at school—lovely flat. I only live in the annex, but it's very like living together and then we always come to Cook's Cove for holidays. I sometimes think it's a mistake."

"Well, it does seem rather—"

"I mean, even families don't spend *all* the time together."

"No fear. My goodness, no." She wondered if she could help herself to some of the bread and butter.

"There's nothing really that we've got in common, you know. She's agnostic; she's always laughed at me. She couldn't bear it when your father sent me books. You should hear her about Roman Catholics. Primrose is quite fearless, you know. She doesn't care what anybody thinks."

"How—marvelous."

She had had no lunch. There had been a restaurant car, but she hadn't been sure she had enough money and thought she might leave it till Harrogate station, but then at Harrogate the next train was in, and at Darlington the refreshment room seemed to be behind bars and only to be for people before they got onto the station or after they had left. At Middlesbrough there had been just time to catch the bus. That was two hours ago.

She tried quietly putting out her hand and was just lifting

the bread up to her teeth when Miss Bowles gave a great gasp, sat bolt upright, clutched the tea table and leaned violently forward, gazing into her face.

"I am absolutely sick of Primrose," she said. "I am utterly, utterly sick of her. You can tell your mother I said so—anyone you like. I hate Primrose Clarke."

"Maids of honor," said the waitress, plonking them down, "two slices Battenberg, two squashed fly. I'll leave you yer bill and put it on the tray as you go. I've got me suppers. Are you better? That's right. Pass up."

"We must go." Miss Bowles stood up and Athene put down the bread and butter again. "Thank you, Winnie, but we must go. What a nice tea. What a shame. We'll come again during the week. My little friend—Mrs. Price's daughter, you know—is staying the week. Let's hope the rain relents." She looked better, almost released. She even managed a watery smile.

"Doesn't she want a bit to eat?"

"Oh, dear, I didn't see you'd done all this. No, I'm afraid we'll have to go. I believe there's going to be something special at home."

"It's scarcely six."

"Six! Oh, my goodness—we must go, Winnie. Come along, Theeny. Goodness, we're so late." She limped out, head rather forward, and stood in the doorway looking at the rain while Athene took issue once more with her luggage.

"Whatever you got there?" asked Winnie.

"A crucifix," said Athene. They smiled at each other. "And a rope ladder."

"That's right," said Winnie. "Likely you'll need the two."

50

Chapter Eight

Primmy was a heavy-looking lady standing at the kitchen sink, which faced the front garden, so that her wide, abstracted face was the first thing they saw as they came up the path. Between them and the face was a gin bottle. A glass stood on the window ledge behind the taps.

The garden was tiny and the gate clicked behind them, but the face did not look up. It went on looking into the sink. Taps were twirled and steam arose. As they entered the cottage there was a great crash of pans.

"Parsley?" said Primmy, spinning round, vigorously drying arms and hands with a tea cloth.

"Oh, I forgot. I'll get it. Er—this is Athie."

"Oh—*I'll* get it. For goodness sake, I'll get it. Might have known. God!"

"This is Theeny."

"Hello. D'you know parsley when you see it?"

"Well, yes. Of course—"

"Then be a good girl and get some. By the gate. Here. Put this hat on." She unhooked a pink mackintosh pixie hood from the back of the door.

"It's all right. I never wear a—"

"The strings tie under your chin. That's better.

"A good handful!" she shouted from the step. "A *good* handful!" And when Athene came back up the path again she found her still there looking at her, holding the latch, swiveling only her eyes as Athene put the parsley on the draining board. She then shut the door and picked up a savage-looking chopper shaped like a crescent moon and fell upon the parsley with considerable noise, pausing once to pour from the gin bottle, then getting down to it again.

"Er—Athie, come over here and get dry," said Sybil, looking at the back of Primrose. "Take off your mac. Are your shoes wet?"

"Oh, nothing. I'm quite all right." She moved to the fireplace and they both stood examining the flames. It was a fireplace of art stonework. Black oval frames, silhouettes of people in periwigs and ruffles hung above it. They had belligerent eighteenth-century faces and hanging jowls, clearly former members of Primmy's family. "That was the *first* Primrose," said Sybil, pointing at one of them, and added in a whisper, "Primrose is in Debrett."

There was a pine settle, a rag rug and a lot of rush-bottomed chairs about. An immense Aga cooker at the kitchen end of the room shone with newness, and along the wall behind it was a parade of copper saucepans in strict order of length and depth. Indoor vines crawled desperately around the windows, trying to get out.

"It's Primmy's cottage," said Sybil loudly. "Isn't it lovely?"

"It's marvelous."

52

They both looked at Primmy's back. The chopping continued.

"You wouldn't recognize it now if you'd seen it before. She knocked walls down—this room was three!—and there was one of those awful iron grates with bars. Think of the black-leading!"

"Oh. Who?"

"It was a fisherman's. She bought it last year. She's a natural with houses. She just has to *step* inside a house to see its possibilities. She knows exactly what to pull down. It is a gift."

"How marvelous."

The conversation flagged. The chopping reached a great crescendo.

"Perhaps—do you think I could unpack and, well, do my hair and so on?" Athene asked at last.

The crescent moon was flung violently down. "No, you can't!" shouted Primrose.

"Oh, Primmy!"

"No, you can't. The reason being, as I've told Bowles again and again, there's nowhere for you *to* unpack. You're sleeping here on the divan. There's no spare drawers, so you'll have to live out of your suitcase."

"Prim! I said I'd sleep here."

"She won't want your rooms. All that stink of liniment. She's not having my room. There isn't another room. She'll be all right here.

"Won't you, Athie?" she asked, all of a sudden pleasant. She scraped the pulverized parsley onto some mushrooms and garlic and, dabbing it all with butter, lovingly slid the dish back into the oven. She picked up her glass, refilled it and came across the room in a business-like way. "Nice dins coming," she said, flopping into a chair. "Let's have a look at you,

Athene Price. Well, you're very good-looking, I'll say that for you." She lit a cigarette. "Nice dress, too. Just about go round one of my thighs, but still. Not much like your mother, are you?"

"Oh, Prim!" A wail from the fireplace.

"Are you like the old man? Good-looking old codger, wasn't he? Met him once. Must have been getting on a bit." She drew on the cigarette as if it were oxygen and she on Nanda Devi. "Only parson I've ever met," she said, coughing, "I'd any time for. Reason being, of course, his heart wasn't in the job." She laughed until she coughed. "Grand chap. Real old cynic."

Athene rose and buttoned up her mackintosh.

"Is your mother over it yet? Not a penny, I suppose?"

Athene walked to the door and picked up her luggage.

"Wonder why parsons have so many children. Maybe they're all cynics. Or just a bit—"

"Goodbye, Miss Bowles," said Athene, "I am going."

"*Athie!* WHERE?"

"I haven't the faintest idea," she said, and went out.

On the path she put down the suitcases and turned back and opened the door again. Sybil was frozen into a monolith; Primrose pouring gin.

"You are the ghastliest woman," she said in a new and surprising voice, a voice that would have needed no oxygen even on Olympus, "the ghastliest woman I have ever met in my whole life."

She slammed the door, fell over the wrought-iron sheep that served as a boot scraper, and went stumbling and running down the rough road to the sea.

Chapter Nine

The man who had painted the pictures in the hotel up the cliff looked out of his window and saw her standing on the quay, her suitcases beside her and all reflected in the wet stones. She stood beside an upturned boat and seemed to be holding on to it. Another wave of fine rain made her bow toward the boat helplessly, though she did not look naturally helpless and had glorious legs. He went to the door.

"I say," he called.

She did not move.

"I say, don't stand there."

She straightened up, but instead of looking at him, picked up her suitcases and began to walk away.

"That's the sea you're going into!" he shouted. "Do you want to commit suicide or something? You'll have a job. It's dead shallow."

She stopped with her back to him and another blast of rain

and spray off the sea set her staggering and soaked him on the step, making him stand back.

"Come in!" he shouted. "I'm not coming out to get you. Come in or drown." He went back into the cottage and looked in the mirror on its nail by the door. Cast down a little by the wiriness of his mustache, he tried to smooth it over with his fingers. He looked out again. So bloody cold. Not a soul stirring. August, for God's sake! Blank windows all round the quay. She had not moved, but it seemed to him there was something less heedless about her back.

"I want to shut the door!" he shouted.

Leaving it open, he went back into the room and stood by the fire. He straightened tubes of paint with his fingertips and swung about on his toes, whistling. He washed a brush vigorously back and forth in a glass of water and took a drawing off a drawing board and let it fall to the floor. He scratched his fingers through his mustache again and polished up his beard, picked up his dirty dinner plate (kippers) from the fender and, hearing her coming up the path, put it in a drawer. He felt excited.

"Don't know who you are or where you've come from," he grumbled about, not looking at her, "with your great luggage and so on. Not been a bus for hours. Been put out of a car, I suppose." He heard the door shut, the cases set down. "You'd better take your mac off and that hat. I can't say I think much of the hat."

"It's . . ." she said. There was a long silence. "It's not mine."

"Sorry for the . . . Shall I hang the mac up? Oh!" She had taken off the hat and he saw her face. "My God!" he said. She looked dazedly round the room and he stood staring. It seemed unlikely that either of them would ever speak again.

"My heaven!" he said at last.

She stared at him and with a great effort, not unbuttoning her dripping mackintosh, said, "I wonder if you could possibly let me have something to eat?"

"Yes. Yes," he said. "Of course you can," but still did not move.

"Anything," she said.

"Anything," he replied. "Yes. Anything. Of course. Kippers?"

"Oh, kippers," she said. "Kippers." Tears filled her eyes. "I would so much love some kippers."

"And tea, perhaps?"

"Tea," she said. "Tea."

"And a bit of bread and butter and so on?"

Tears flowed down her cheeks.

He began to rush about, filling a huge iron saucepan with water, scuffling in paper bags. He was fiftyish, fat, gray-haired, rather red-lipped, light on his feet, apparently clumsy with his hands. The room was chaotic, clothes dropped on every chair, dishes stacked about the floor, two card tables covered with paints and painters' belongings in heaps. Books and papers lay on all flat surfaces, open and shut. The smell of linseed oil and many meals was strong. In a huge, unblacked, cast-iron grate blazed an enormous fire, steaming the windows. "I'm in a bit of a mess," he said as she took off her coat, and stood gazing at her, half closing his eyes, loaf in one hand, knife in the other.

"Could I cut it?"

"Cut it?"

"Just cut a bit of bread?"

"Oh, yes. Yes, of course." He held them out.

"I'm sorry. I'm most dreadfully hungry. I've been traveling all day. I've kept on sort of missing meals."

"Great mistake at your age." He tried to return to his first ferocity, but it ebbed away as he saw her fingers buttering. "My God," he said, "you're beautiful. How old . . ."

"What?" She was munching hard.

"Nothing." The kettle began to scream and he brought her tea. He poured himself some, first turning the mug upside down to see if it were empty. He sat on the fender and drinking tea, watched her.

"Might the kippers . . . ?"

"Yes, shall—?"

"I can."

She got up and drained off the kippers onto a plate, found a knife and fork and ran them under the tap and dried them on her handkerchief. She sat down and began to eat.

"You're eating bones," he said.

"I don't care." She took a haunch of bread, a gulp of tea and fell upon the kippers again.

When she had finished she sighed and sat back and for the first time looked straight at him. She felt brave as Hercules.

"Oh, my word," she said. "Oh, my goodness," and started laughing.

"What is it?"

"You—oh, my goodness! If you knew!"

"Knew what?"

"Oh—where I've been. What I've seen."

Something in his face made her stop. He was pinning some paper onto a drawing board.

"Sit still," he said. "Just like that. No, leave your hair alone. Don't move." He started drawing.

"Can I—" she said presently.

"No. Take off your shoes."

She kicked them off.

58

"Take off your stockings."

"Why . . ." But she took them off. They lay in two sad pinkish heaps at her feet, like dead roses.

"I want your wet feet," he said. It grew quite dark outside and he switched on a spotlight and made up the fire, saying, "No, don't move yet." He threw the first drawing down and started again. She found as the fire blazed up and the rain and wind shook the window and the sea rushed and roared upon the quay that she was in great content. She felt her head settle against the high back of the horsehair armchair and her eyes begin to close.

"Wake up," he said sharply. "Don't fall asleep yet."

"I must go and find somewhere to sleep," she said drowsily.

"Nonsense," he said. "You're sleeping here."

Chapter Ten

It was seven a.m.

"Now then, what about this, then?" said the postman.

Winnie took the letters and looked them through. Then she stepped out and stood beside the postman in the road. Outside the gate on the cliff top they lifted their faces up to see the sky.

"Aye," said Winnie, "it's holding off."

"It's grand."

"Improving."

"Wey—it's a bobby-dazzler. September!"

"Nay, it's not September yet."

"It's got bit September int, though."

"Aye."

They stood about in the cold, bright air. Below them the bay was filled up and leveled off with mist like egg-white in a cup, but all around the cliff edge each blade of grass and bramble leaf shone in the dazzling sunshine. Orange berries looked polished against the ugly red wall of the hotel. The shabby tables and chairs on the lawn, soaked almost to pulp by the week of rain, took the light like furniture of heaven. Birds sang and as the sun rose higher a sharpness in the air enlivened even the hard fists of the chrysanthemums so that one realized that they might turn to flowers. There was a wonderful smell of rain and grass, undreamed of yesterday.

"Yesterday!" said the postman.

"Bye," said Winnie with a long, disgusted look.

"Yesterday were some day, all right. What d'you do wi' your lot a day like yon?"

"Guests?" said Winnie. "They went to bed, mostly. We had two casuals in for a tea which they didn't eat."

"It gets you down, days like yesterday."

"Aye. Well. They'll benefit today. I'd best get on. I've got me breakfasts."

"Aye, and I've me rounds down int bottom. Pity I can't just throwt sack down amongst 'em." He looked toward the bay. The invisible sea swished between thoughtful pauses.

"Looks as though you've had a post already," he said, for a parcel seemed to be lying beside the gate, a damp and ugly parcel with four knobs and a label on it.

"Hello," said Winnie, striding over and picking it up. "It's not for no one 'ere," she said after a minute. "Now, I wonder who int world . . ."

"It's a queer-looking affair," said the postman. "It's not come through any regular channel."

"It just says 'Sybil.' "

"That's p'raps Miss Bowles. It's a rare queer shape, like one o' them crosses full of 'oles you puts on graves—a rare heavy un. Mebbe it's lead. Shall I tek it down?"

"No," said Winnie and looked thoughtfully at the day. "I'll just hold on til't a bit and see what transpires."

She stood after he had left, looking in front of her as if waiting for someone. A curtain was pulled back behind her and the pasty face of a guest peered out at the day. There was a rattle of teacups being turned the right way up in the dining room, but she still didn't move. Ten eggs. Ten rashers. Time yet.

In the distance there came the noise of a car. It grew louder and rocketed up the lane, spun round the bus stop and pulled up on the asphalt turning space. Primrose fell out of it and marched on stout legs toward her, followed by Miss Bowles. Primrose looked formidable, brisk and fit, a Dunkirk of a woman: Miss Bowles, who had yesterday seemed to Winnie to be a wreck, now looked as if yesterday had been golden.

"Coffee, Winnie? Any hope?" called Primrose, passing by and off into the dining room. Miss Bowles, as she reached her, placed a long hand on Winnie's arm. "Oh, Winnie," she said.

Still Winnie stood, and after a while the top of the postman's hat was seen rising up the side of the cliff, followed by the rest of him.

"Another funny thing," he said. "There's a great rope ladder down yonder hangin' from a bedroom winder."

Chapter Eleven

"I suppose one would know," she thought.

She was tramping steadily up a long, winding road between woodlands in the early afternoon. She had no luggage, bare legs, and was wearing a mackintosh. Her hands were in her pockets and in one was a purse. Under the mackintosh was a cardigan and a nightdress, and under the nightdress was not much except Athene.

One might not know. You did hear of things. Old Mrs. Arrowsmith had even had a baby and not known it was there. Just all of a sudden woosh—Jimmie Arrowsmith. She was a huge, fat woman. It had been very disgusting.

How could one know? I was terribly tired. I went to sleep in a chair. I woke up in a bed. I ran downstairs and picked up my shoes and mac and ran upstairs again and locked the door. There wasn't one sound.

I went to sleep in the chair after the kippers. While he was drawing. I must have been mad.

Would one know?

The sun slanted through the trees, and the shadows of the trees sometimes lay in bars across the winding drive. She stepped in and out of them, in darkness, then in light, but marching steadily, firm and fast. I can see cardigan cuffs under the wrists of my mac and I can feel my nightie hitched up under my mac. I did put on my nightie, but I don't think I went to bed exactly. I sat for ages on the bed. Then there was the ladder to fix. But that was when it was nearly light. I don't know really what happened at all.

He was such an ugly man. When he bent down to the fire there was pink in the middle of his hair. He had pursy lips. Oh, heavens—what happened? It wasn't as if one had been drinking wine.

Left, right, on she went. The sun was like lamplight behind the trees. Birds were quiet.

Thinking hard, she remembered the bilberries. She had been sitting for ages without her stockings, lying back in the chair, and only his breathing and whistling through his (oh, Lord) lips. It had grown less stormy outside and they had heard footsteps—two firm footsteps, one lighter footstep and one long, trailing footstep.

"What's that?" She had sat upright.

He had whistled on through his teeth.

"It's people coming. It's Miss Bowles. I can hear her foot."

Standing back from the drawing, examining it with one eye shut, he had stood up, leaned back and switched off the spotlight. "Dum, dum, dum," he had sung, and still looking at the drawing from his arm's length, he had flung open a door behind him. "In there," he had said.

There was a knock. She scuttled over and he shut her in.

"Cleopatra. CleoPATra, proceedeth out of Egypt," she had heard him sing. "CLEOPATRA—" There was the sound of agitation at the front door. She listened in the dark of the tiny room she seemed to be in—a stone floor. Something dripping.

"Simply disappeared," she heard Miss Bowles exclaim. "Simply walked out . . . Not at the hotel . . . No buses since . . ."

Rumble rumble from the man.

A bark (Primrose). "You are sure now, Basil?"

(Basil. Oh goodness!)

More rumbling, rustling and a slam. Silence. Utter silence. The man had gone out with them. She opened the door a little—her hand had not left the latch—and looked out at the room with its center light—bulb without a shade—switched on, killing the firelight, the comforting shadows, the sweeping mahogany back of the horsehair chair. In the glare there was only squalor now, squalor and her stockings on the floor. She stood gazing at them with mounting disgust. Hadn't they seen them? Or the suitcases behind the door? Presumably not. Feeling about, she switched on the light in the little room she stood in, for the dripping was growing insistent.

It was a pantry with stone shelves and on the shelves were the most appalling things: green bread, bits of stew surmounted by forests, blue pieces of old onion, a shoe, bottles and bottles all over the floor, some terrible potatoes with bending long white shoots coming out of them, and, by her face, a glass dish of stewed bilberries tilted up by an unmentionable-looking bundle of meat in stained newspaper and spilling in a long, pouring stream, drip, dripping down the wall.

The flagstones beneath her feet, the fine stone walls spelled home. She knew them and the folk they were meant for—plain-living folk, frugal, excellent. Near such a pantry Emily Brontë had stood, chaste as a willow, kneading elastic bread, her German grammar propped up before her, old Biddy in the rocking chair, Charlotte and Anne peeling the potatoes. Drip drip drip. The blood-red abandoned mess denied all. She had cried, "Oh, where have I got to? Where am I going?" She could remember no more.

Tramp, tramp.

Yes, she could. If she tried. She had grown wild. He had come back in alone and shut the door and tried to put a kettle on and she had raved about. He had stood quite helpless as she rolled her head about against the awful wall. He had said, "Well, I'd better take you back, then."

"No! No!"

"They're all right. Just schoolma'ams. They're dead worried. I'll tell them I've found you. Come on, I'll take you back." He had seemed quite frightened.

"I'm not going. I'm not going anywhere. I've nowhere to go. They may have had T.B. and been drunks and no money," she had wailed. (His jaw fell.) "But they had a home. They always had somewhere to go."

She remembered being got up the stairs (they were in a cupboard) and put on a bed. Then her cases had been brought up. How he had puffed. He had left them by the bed and made snuffling noises. Then he had gone out quietly, stood for a while creaking on the landing and at last quietly shut the door.

She was sure he had. He had shut the door. He had gone out. She was quite sure.

But had he come back? How would one know? Surely one would know? Can one stop being a virgin and not know?

On she tramped and the trees thinned and she was looking down on Auntie Boo's school in the afternoon light.

66

Chapter Twelve

Part 1, Sub. Sect. 1. Page 1.

My name is Beams, short for Moonbeams (big glasses), Phoebe at the font. Ugly as sin. Alas for me.

I am at present staying in Wales with the Padshaws. I care nothing for the Padshaws and the Padshaws care nothing for anybody. What they care about—all they care about—is things like caulking, tacking and drying facilities. They have a boat. They worship this boat. It is a most interesting thing to observe, this boat worship, and I have already made a small study of it anthropologically. I intend to become a psychiatrist eventually but at present I am studying anthropology as I believe that psychiatrists get pressed for time.

The Padshaws live in a midland town. Mr. Padshaw is a doctor. I am glad that I am not his patient because he never stops bellowing and laughing and booming about. It must be awful if you aren't feeling well.

"It's me back, Doctor."

BOOM BOOM.

"I've got this pain around the 'eart."

BELLOW BELLOW.

"My head's that bad."

CRASH SLAP HURRAH.

They are the most frightfully healthy family, with rosy, open faces and when they're pleased with each other they shout out, "Oh, good MAN!" Whatever sex. I sit brooding at them and cracking my knuckle bones, hoping to rouse up a bit of distaste. I never do. "Good old Beams," they cry, "what about a trip in the dinghy? A swim around the bay?" I go wandering off and sit on the sea wall and throw pebbles at other pebbles on the beach pretending I am God going for Dr. Padshaw.

One day I was sitting there and Bobby Padshaw came along. (They're all B. Very appropriate. Billy, Bobby, Bunty and Baby. Mrs. is Bess and Dr. P is Boofie. Yes.) Bobby Padshaw came along and said, "I say, Beams, why don't you try and be a bit less difficult?" I said, "I'm not difficult, I'm impossible," and I lifted my upper lip in a haughty and disdainful manner exposing quite an area of gum.

As I say, I have recently completed an anthropological survey of the Padshaws and boat worship. It is called *Padshaw-Hoo* (or *Padshaw-Ho*). It is rather short as there aren't any books here to look things up except for some very queer medical ones of Dr. Padshaw's which he shows to other midland friends in other holiday cottages after they've all been drinking beer and everyone falls about. Otherwise it's Mary Webb, Frances Parkinson Keyes, belonging to Mrs., and the most terrible stuff belonging to the children—Georgette Heyer, Gene Stratton Porter and Arthur Mee.

I have decided therefore that I shall pass the rest of the holiday writing an analytical study, a sort of case history of

68

someone, to pass the time. After all, I intend to pass the rest of my life in this sort of way, so I may as well get started.

I began with Mrs. Padshaw. I watched her through meals, mentally noting and evaluating her nervous habits. It was not very fruitful because she has none. Honestly. I don't think I ever saw a human being more lacking in a nervous system. She just sits there, through meal after meal, jaw rotating, great big face. Just looking ahead over the chicken pilaff. She's very large (All the Padshaws are large. Giant-like. Particularly the baby) and Mrs. P's eyes are round and blue and gaze at nothing. She is an absolutely confident woman. Munch, munch. Round and round. Not a flicker. She hasn't asked me a single question since I came. I don't think she knows my name. Neither does Dr. P. He asked me yesterday if I thought the boat was an improvement on last time and I said I hadn't been before. (They ask a lot of children here.) "Haven't you?" he yelled. "Good God, I thought B brought you last year. Well, well." Off he went, roaring and booming. He calls me Batty. He hasn't got much in the way of a nervous system either. I can crack my knuckles and pick my midge bites for hours and hours and they don't even SEE.

The other night it was hot and I couldn't sleep and I got out of bed and hung out of the window and I heard Bess and Boofie—i.e. Dr. & Mrs. P—talking about me in bed in the room next to mine.

"Hardly a beauty. Chinless, poor thing."

"Is she fourpence in the shilling?"

"Good God, no. Rather bright, isn't she—isn't she the brainy one?"

"Old parents."

"Ah!"

"Took a risk. About a hundred, wasn't he?"

I wrote it all down as it is revealing analytically though all I could think of at the time was thank goodness Athene isn't here, hanging out of this window listening too—it being so desperate for her because she allows herself no feelings.

I had then the most sudden and unexpected and violent rush of emotion for Athene, which I am also noting. I suddenly saw my sister Athene's face looking at me all calm and still from the barn window when Seb and I went together through the raspberries and her eyes quite lost as she gazed. Ridiculous because I am sure that when Seb and I left the barn and went over the courtyard and through the back kitchen door, past the tea towels, we never turned and looked back. I remember seeing a great fat thrush sitting on a post, its beak all juice, not even bothering to fly away. I do remember that. But I never looked back at the barn. So this definition—face—gazing at me from the barn slit, high up over the sea, with the moon lighting up all the ghastly boats and buoys and bits of rope and arty fishing nets ordered from all the best shops—this face can only have been engendered by sentimentality.

But I saw it so clear that I said, "Oh, Athene," and I heard the Padshaws next door say, "Eh? What was that?" and then, "Hello—someone awake there?" loud enough to wake the fishes in the deep. But no sound further.

To my distaste, I found that my face was all wet and my vision impeded. The sea and the sky and the quay began to swim into a great merging flood and had I had a chin it would no doubt have trembled.

Athene's face disappeared and I felt tears drop onto my hands from out of my eyes—an unusual experience. Then two more dropped and I heard Boofie's voice, drowsy now, say, "Oh well, poor little sod," and at this most unpleasant expression the tears immediately ceased and with very systematic control I crawled into my sleeping bag and fell asleep with a very cool expression on my face.

It rained the next day so hard that even the Padshaws got a bit downcast and all set off to the pictures in Rhyll. The baby went too, not to the pictures but to Rhyll where its mother has a friend she was going to cadge tea off while the rest of them went to sit through whatever was on at the local, steaming in their oilskins. Great fun for the rest of the audience. They left me because I said I wasn't allowed to go to the pictures (I do tend toward lying) because of my eyes and they didn't ask any more questions. (What a doctor.)

I share a bedroom with the baby. I started with Bunty, who is in my form at school though we're not friends. I know she didn't want me to come. I think Mother asked. She met the Padshaws last Speech Day and Mrs. knows someone or other of Mother's—some funny friend of Miss Bowles who has a mustache and emotional scenes. Well, anyway, I was sort of invited because I had nowhere else to go and of course I had a row with Bunty the very first night (she says I grind my teeth) and I moved in with the baby, who yells and makes dreadful noises under its blankets and dribbles all down its obscene, all-in-one pajamas. There is always its pot standing right in the middle of the bedroom floor. Always. Night and day.

After they had gone I found that I could not write my report—I had decided to get down to one on Athene—in that bedroom, and wandering round the cottage I found I couldn't write it anywhere. "Come, come," I said, "irrational emotionalism. A useful psychiatrist must be above and beyond his surroundings." But I just couldn't be and in the end I pulled on some oilskins and went over and got into the boat. In the cabin it was all right.

It was in fact most pleasant. I lit the stove. The rain rattled

71

down and the boat slip-slopped about. I took comfort from the rocking movement and enclosed warmth (womb) and found myself feeling better than for ages. I ate some chocolate Seb had given me, took off my glasses which had got all steamed up, feeling that in these surroundings I might do well, weak though I might be.

It is worth noting, anyhow, that psychiatrists are a pretty weak lot and I should know, having been humped round half a dozen of them in my time. Nor are they above their surroundings. They are absolute and utter reflections of their surroundings. In fact, if you ask me, put a psychiatrist in some surroundings and he'll start scratting and stirring them about like a dog in a basket until they have been molded into his own precise and particular shape.

Take the first one—Mrs. Winterschladen. I was six. January, bitter cold, and in the war, so no petrol and we had to take the bus. All the way to Leeds. We changed about five times and we were thoroughly, utterly frozen by the time we got there. They told me I was going to see a doctor about my eyes but I knew that it was really about Miss Battersoft's outburst.

You see (this is a bore, but I think that it is analytically enlightening to the report I am about to make on Athene and the sibling troubles to which she has been exposed)—you see Miss Battersoft was the new teacher at the village school where I'd been for a year and she was very young and clever and well trained (like our dog) and everyone went on about how lucky we were to have her in such a small country place.

Well, she soon had us all sorted out. I remember the first day. In she comes. "*Now* then." Eyes darting here and there. "Stand *up*, if you please. Who is that child with the bulge in the cheek? Thank you, I will take charge of this." (Opens up stove, drops in Ellie Longstaff's halfpenny chew, then Billy Norton's dead mouse.) "I dare say it *didn't* belong to you. Yes, I dare say it does smell. Stand up straight when you're spoken to . . ." etc.

By the end of the first term she had us all chanting our tables, doing fractions. Even little Willie Ollershaw who used to fall asleep at the back every day—he's dead now—she had him up in the front reading his *Jem had ten hens in a pen* like the rest of us.

The rest that is except the Rector's daughter. For there was I somehow quite unable to get the hang of anything. I knew the letters and the numbers. It was just I didn't seem able to do anything with them. She moved me up to the front too, saying that I'd not have any excuse then about not being able to see.

But actually I could see all right. I could see for instance fantastically well out of the window and this was the trouble. The school was at the end of the rectory garden and I could see Mother sometimes trotting round the flower beds and sometimes a duster shaken out of a window and our dovecote, all mossy with the cat asleep along the top of it. I had a very good time gazing around. She carried on at me but it did no good. I wasn't the sort of child to cry or it would have been all right. She would have been used to that all right. But my being so ugly and young—Ath and Seb being so good-looking and old—I had to look around for better weapons than tears, and I found them. Words.

I suppose being in a house like ours I just picked up a lot of words and ways of putting them, and being naturally not a very pleasant character as I was always being reminded, I was easily able to lash out with them AS WITH A WHIP.

One day I said something apparently so awful—I think it was when she said I wasn't trying and I said on the contrary I was very trying—that she went suddenly into a very disturbed and wrought condition. In fact she suddenly went all wet and queer round the mouth and got hold of her desk lid and began to slam it up and down and give out little moans and pants. I felt terribly that I must help her. I think in fact that it was at this precise moment when Miss Battersoft had the brainstorm that I knew that I wanted to be a psychiatrist—though I don't suppose I would have put it quite like that then, being six. I went up to her desk and touched her arm and she went Honk, honk, honk, grrrrrrrrh. "Please," I said, "Miss Battersoft, Daddy always says count ten."

Then she ran from the room, over the schoolyard, over the rectory lawn where father was in the sweet peas. "I'm going," she shrieked (unnecessarily), "I'm off," and she vanished into her Austin Seven and was never seen again.

So they took me to Leeds to see Mrs. Winterschladen, who was an "eye doctor"! I went with Father and Auntie Boo, because at the last minute Mother couldn't come because of Seb getting measles or something. She wasn't over keen anyway, I think, and as for Father he was absolutely dead set against. It was Auntie Boo and various very clever friends of various people and the letter Miss Battersoft wrote from Welwyn Garden City where she lived with her mother (and I bet *she* was a wreck) that made him agree. At any rate that's the feeling I have.

Auntie Boo, who is very commanding, decided to come with Father and me because she suspected we'd never get there by ourselves and just go off to a tea shop or listen to a concert (My father took me to a concert when I was five. Sooner than Athie) and she put on her Red Cross commandant's uniform to make it all more serious.

Well—Mrs. Winterschladen lived not in a hospital or in an

oculist's shop but in a small semi-detached red brick house on the outskirts of Leeds. It was snowing when we arrived and darkish, but even so you could see it wasn't a very happy place at any time. The upstairs windows had the curtains drawn over them, the gate had lost its catch and had a bit of string in a loop that didn't work, and there were all kinds of things lying about the garden in the snow—old boxes, rusty biscuit tins, holes in the ground and a really very nice tricycle on its back, all being snowed on. The door needed a coat of paint.

So did Mrs. Winterschladen. She was wild and fat and her dress was lacking a button. She held a cup of tea in her hand and had an excitable moving eye. My father, who had already at the gate said, "Oh, whatever is all this!" now had to turn away and survey the sky above Leeds with a sort of god-like withdrawal. Auntie Boo did the introductions. "Yes, yes," said Mrs. Winterschladen, putting down the cup of tea on the end of the banisters. She gathered me in and with wafting movements shooed Auntie Boo and Father away.

"What's this?" cried Father, spinning round.

"Collect in two hours," said Mrs. W.

"Indeed no!"

"Yes, yes, all children are happy with me."

"No," said Father, and "Excuse me one minute," said Boo, thrusting her shoulders forward so that all her Red Cross emblems gleamed.

They made a formidable pair.

But the door closed and they were left on the step. I don't know what they did because I was led off inside into the untidiest room I have ever seen in my life. I love untidy rooms usually—not like Athie, who's always putting paper clips into envelopes marked paper clips and straightening out the fire tongs. I love our nursery for instance, with Seb and Father's trains all over the floor and my papers about; or the kitchen, with Mother putting the flour bin in the rocking chair and ducks looking in the door and the clothes horse over the fire with the airing clothes smelling lovely and me sitting inside it all warm and wheezy. I love untidiness.

But that room! It wasn't busy, or warm, or comforting. It was *frantic*. It was a frantic place in which was no peace.

She sat down and tried to look motherly and comfortable and you've never seen such a tight dress. I made conversation as best I could, suggesting that perhaps we might tidy up a bit before she started on my eyes. "Eyes?" she said, after she'd turned purple and black and then back to crimson (well, surely no one could *like* being in that mess). "Eyes? No, darling, first we're going to play some games," and she suddenly fired a ball at me from some hidden cranny (though there weren't many) and I fell to the ground. Honestly it reminded me of air raids. When I had picked myself up she was writing busily in a notebook. "Let's do a little dance," she said, and began clapping her hands and slowly jogging round the table to the tune of "Girls and Boys Come Out to Play." I said it wasn't right and she stopped alertly and said, "Ah? Don't you like going out to play?" and I said yes of course I did but she'd got the time wrong, and I sang it right. She gave me a look and dashed back to her book, attacking it with great vigor.

Then she tried to make me draw a lot of shapes (which I couldn't) and do a lot of sums (which I couldn't) and then she showed me a lot of pictures where I had to point out things I couldn't see and she made a great fuss about it all being great fun really and then wrote very earnestly in the book for hours and hours.

"Tell me," she said at last, and I remembered what Auntie Boo is always saying: A dirty man never smells as bad as a dirty woman—"Tell me, Phoebe darling, does Mummy love Daddy, do you think?" I remember so well the sort of hopeful look in her eyes that I can't believe it was six whole years ago. "Is Mummy *happy* with Daddy, do you think?"

Well, I don't know why I said it. I just stood there and said, "A dirty man never smells as bad as a dirty woman," and she flung me out and shrieked for her daughter to come and take me away and I spent the rest of the time watching this awful girl doing ballet steps in a tutu with a tear in it.

When Father and Boo came back there were raised voices in the hall and I was whisked away and taken to the most expensive, marvelous, smashing restaurant near Leeds bus station where they gave me absolutely everything I wanted— pork pie, H.P. Sauce, chips, tinned pears, jam tart, condensed milk and tea, and when I asked at the end for more chips my father said, "Yes, she SHALL HAVE more chips" and went and got them for me himself. In the bus he sat me on his knee and neither of us mentioned Mrs. Winterschladen. Auntie Boo was sitting at the back, very stern and upright—the bus very crowded.

It was a dark, cold, cold journey in the blackout, but Daddy played I Spy and it was surprising how much you could see if you tried. Other people joined in. There was one workman really good, I remember. When we got on the last bus and near home I drowsed off and only woke up once. I remember I said it was an awful shame about Mrs. Winterschladen's little girl's toys not being looked after and Daddy said yes, he was very sorry for Mrs. Winterschladen's little girl. I said I was very sorry for Mrs. Winterschladen, but he said, in a very clear voice, no, he wasn't sorry for her. He was not sorry for her, he said, in the very least.

So I didn't decide on my career as a result of that visit.

During the next few years I visited a number of other people, but I don't remember them very clearly. It always seemed a waste of time and nothing ever came of it except bills. At school children came and went and there sat Beams, still at the same desk at the front "because of her eyes," still "making no progress," often falling asleep. I'd got glasses now, very thick and large, and was henceforth Phoebe no more. That was something.

It was, however, all because I couldn't play games and I couldn't learn music and I couldn't even paint because I kept getting the lines in the wrong places. All the still-lifes of apples and tins and books they stuck up—hopeless. There was a kind old lady teaching us now who had actually taught most of the mothers of the village children and she often fell asleep too, especially after the dinner hour, and we all ran riot until Father or someone came thundering in. In the evenings they all read to me. Father whenever I asked, Mother when she could, Athene when she wasn't in a dream, Seb never because he was embarrassed reading to a great fat nine-year-old. They'd say, "All right, we'll read to you if you'll just read to us—just one line," and I'd say, "Yes, yes, only do start." After a while they'd say, "Now then, Beams, come on, you—" and there would be the great page in front of me and I'd start spelling out and they'd say, "No, no—see it as a whole. . . . No, Beams, come on, surely you can read that. You could read 'this' and 'him' when you were five."

Then off I would go—storms and rages. Rushing from the room.

"Let her go. It's hopeless. I don't know what we're going to do with her." (Seb)

"There's certainly something wrong." (Athie)

"It's no good my trying." (Mother)

And then Father, of course, "Let her be."

Then one day when I was nine and a half Auntie Posie was staying. I love Auntie Posie. She never never tries to help. She never makes her own bed or washes a dish or offers to shop for Mother. She's rich. She's never thought about it. Duties get done, she seems to think. She sits and sits looking very pleased to be wherever she is. After a bit you don't notice her hardly—you carry on all round her, having quarrels and talking rubbish and acting the goat, and she always looks delighted unless Seb is really going for me or I am kicking him and perhaps biting simultaneously. And then she just looks slightly anxious for a time instead.

One day for some reason I was in the drawing room at home making a box. The others were all out and I had brought my nails and planks indoors to be sociable with Auntie P. I used to make a lot of things in those days which needed a lot of bashing and hammering. They said, Oh well, it stops her quarreling.

Bash, bash, bash, bash, bash, bash, I went. Pause. Sound of birds, hesitant twitters across the lawn. Buzz of bees. Then bash, bash, bash, bash, bash bash—

"Beams."

—bash, bash.

"Beams dear."

"Yes?"

"Would you like a game?"

"No, thanks, Auntie P."

"Sure, dear?"

—bash, bash bash.

"Beams dear—"

"Yes?"

"Why not read a book, or—"

79

"Don't be silly."

"Oh." (She'd forgotten.)

"You know I can't read a book. Never will."

"Oh, yes, dear. Yes, you will."

Bash, bash—

"Beams, Beams—"

Silence.

"I couldn't read until I was ever so old."

"Did you mind?"

"Oh, yes."

"Did it come all of a sudden?"

She looked over at me with her big, flat, silly, loving eyes. "Oh, yes."

The last person I went to see was a very important man at Newcastle. They didn't tell me until just before and then they tried sweetening it up a bit. "We thought we'd go and see another eye man, dear. Perhaps on Tuesday."

(Perhaps; they'd known for weeks.)

"You seem to have plenty of money," I said. "Why don't you burn it on a fire?"

There was the usual—a sort of exasperated, sad silence. They'd not argued with me for ages. I hardly talked to them now. I went climbing trees right up to the top and held the top, thin twigs in my fingertips and swung myself about and my feet turned to water. At first they tried to stop me. Now they knew it was no good. Nor was it any good trying to make me wash my hair or stop eating my fingernails. When we all went to church on Sunday I used to sit backward in the pew and rest my face with my great big specs on the back and moon round at all the old ladies and widen out my mouth like a frog until they all got uncomfortable. I used to wince, too, when they hit the wrong notes but never join in myself. I used to fling myself about and put my tongue out at Seb when he went by carrying the cross, nose in the air, all Holy Jo. When Father preached I made a great thing of going to sleep. They all used to say in the village, "That little un's a bit foony." "Looks like a mad chemist." "Looks like it were grown in a bottle." I tried not to disappoint them.

When I got to Newcastle, it was a hospital—no toys on the lawn—and they made me do a lot of intelligence tests which were extremely boring, and then they said I had to go into a waiting room. It was a nice waiting room with comfortable chairs and a desk and a gramophone and a fire and an old man asleep on a sofa. I pottered about a bit and started messing on the gramophone, and out burst the New World Symphony at the top of its voice.

The old man sprang up and said, "Hey? What?" and I said, "Hush. Listen," and we listened for ages and he said, "Heard it before, have you?" and I said, "Of course." "Know what it's called?" I told him and he said, "How d'you know?" I said, "I do. Anyway, it'll be on the label" and when it stopped I showed him and said, "Look. New World Symphony. By Dvorak." He said, "That's right. Are you Phoebe Price?"

"I'm Beams Price."

"Are you the one that thinks she can't read?"

"I can't."

"Well, you just have."

"No, I haven't," I said. "We've got that record at home. I know the look of the label."

"Go on," he said, "read this one."

"I can't," I said.

"Well," he said, "listen to it."

I listened and said, "Oh, please—please, what is it?"

"Read it," he said.

I read "The Emp— The Emperor."

"O.K.," he said. "You can read. You'll read fine soon. Go home."

"Can I have it?" I asked, grabbing it.

"No."

"I must, I must."

"Learn manners," he said, and I went up to him and I remember I took a good deep breath and breathed a few times afterward and said with the most terrific charm you can possibly imagine, it might have been Athie, mouth stuck out all plums, "Excuse me, sir, but if this record belongs to you could I please take it home? I promise to send you the money—or my father might pay for it, he's outside. But whatever happens I promise I would send it as soon as I get home after seeing the doctor."

"All right," he said. "Take it. Off you go. You've seen the doctor."

Well, of course it was rubbish because I couldn't read when I got home. I could read no better than when I'd set out. They were all disappointed. But believe it or not I found that I could read about a fortnight later. I started casually reading out this and that and at first they pretended they hadn't noticed, though I knew they were really wild with excitement. After about a month I was reading all day—even when listening to The Emperor. I found that I could read even with The Emperor at full blast, and I could read in the bath or in church or up a tree or walking through the village in the pouring rain and all the book dye coming out onto your mac (red is the worst). Not a single soul said, "There, I told you so," not even Auntie P—though I wouldn't have minded. I believe the old man at Newcastle had given them all some sort of a blasting and told them to stop worrying about me. Rather unkind, really.

From this time my attention was quite fixed upon the profession of Psychiatry and it has not been even momentarily distracted.

Finishing, Beams felt very pleased and turned to the first page of the exercise book and wrote *Introduction.* She then turned back, ruled it all off and wrote: *Section 1, Athene Price, 16 years, 11 months.*

Then she looked out of the porthole for a moment and saw a very wet telegraph boy hammering at the Padshaws' cottage door. She opened the port and called, "Hello."

"Telegram," he shouted back.

"For Padshaw?"

"For Price."

"For *Price?* All right, I'm coming. Hang on."

IS A THIN PADSHAWS RING COOK'S COVER 37 URGENT BOWLES.

"Thanks," she said. "It doesn't make sense."

The telegraph boy said that the postmistress had been of the same opinion and perhaps it was a code.

"I suppose I'd better, though," she said. "Can I have a lift on your crossbar?"

He said, looking at her hips, that no, there was a phone box down the lane, so she tramped off there, dug out some money and, being Beams, telephoned not the Cook's Cove number but Sebastian's.

Unsuccessfully, however, and after thinking and sighing she managed in a few minutes to get Primrose's cottage and was told by Sybil not to worry after all.

"It's all right. We've just heard. Athie's gone to your aunt's.

83

There's been a little muddle. We're so ashamed at the panic. So sorry, Beams dear. Are you all right? Having a nice summer?"

"Glorious," said Beams, ringing off. The Padshaws' truck passed by, bursting with jolly children and the sound of communal song.

"And it'll be health foods for supper, I wouldn't wonder," she said to her face, reflected in the rainy glass.

Chapter Thirteen

"Excuse me, is that the Buddhist monastery?"

"No."

"Oh. Isn't it Kilpatrick 838?"

"Yes."

"But isn't it a Buddhist monastery?"

"No."

"I was given this number. It's very important."

"This is the Society of Saint Matthew."

"Oh. I know he *said* Buddhists."

"I am very sorry, madam. This is an Anglican community for men. Good afternoon.

"Queer," he said, lying back in his chair in the hall.

"What?" said Sebastian.

"Some nut-case female wanting a Buddhist monastery."

"Are you coming to do the bees?"

"Must I?"

"All right, don't." Sebastian marched off, collecting a straw skep on the way and some long gloves.

"Wait," Lucien called, "I'm coming." They went together to the apiary, where several monks were already working. "Over there," said one, nodding toward a great black hanging drip of something like Christmas pudding on a sycamore branch.

"Help," said Seb.

"All right," said the monk, tucking a veil into his habit neck, "just as you like. Help granted."

"No. It's all right. I've got to take one someday."

"Are you sure? Swarms are swarms. The vast majority don't feel the need."

"No, I must. I'm scared stiff."

"Wrong reason. That's pride."

"I dare say. I'll take it, though. Lucien, hold the branch and when I say now, give it a good hoik."

One or two other monks appeared from among the rows of beehives like ghosts stepping out of tombs. "Watch it, laddie," said one, "it's a grand big swarm."

Lucien had got in behind it, between the swarm and the trunk. The bees were growling quietly, only a few unsettled ones vibrating round its edges. Its sides were bumpy and glossy like a brown pineapple. You could have cut a slice.

"They're safe as houses," called old Father Ignatius. "Once they're in the swarm they're not concerned with you and me."

"All forty thousand of them," called Brother Geoffrey. "I knew a chap once who got a swarm on his head." Lucien moaned. "Had to stand still for days."

"Look, Lucien hasn't got his head covered," said Father Ignatius angrily, and Lucien moaned again. "Get on, can't you?" he called to Seb.

"They'd not get through yon great black thicket," said someone.

"You're jealous," said Brother Geoffrey.

"*Now!*" shouted Seb. Lucien yoiked and the big, dark lump fell into the skep with a fizzy, tumbling plop.

"Always reminds me of horses," said Brother Geoffrey.

"That's enough now," said Father Ignatius, cackling.

Seb bundled up the swarm in the skep, windmilling away the odd bee. "With my compliments," he bowed, holding the forty thousand in his arms. "What'll I do with them?"

"Give them here," said Brother Geoffrey. "In the barrow. I've a hive ready. Do you want to see them walk in?"

"Where's Lucien gone?"

"Over the hills and far away, his hair flowing behind him. You'd better go after him. Isn't he on reception anyway? Doing the phone?"

"No, he'd finished."

"Oh, well, you're both free till Sext."

"I'll hive them for you if you like. I can do that. My father let me."

"No. No need. Go and collapse. And well done," he called as Seb went striding away toward the apiary wall, bouncing with pleasure on the balls of his feet.

He found Lucien sitting on the edge of the pea field, getting imaginary bees out of his hair.

"We're free till Sex," he announced, dropping down beside him. Muffled oaths came out of Lucien's curtained face.

"It's funny—"

"Got one!" said Lucien. "I knew there was one. Ow! Oh, hell, it's got me. Lord, I hate bees."

"It's funny, Lucien."

"What is?"

"I'd have thought that hilarious a couple of weeks ago."

"Uh?"

87

"Being free till Sex. I'd have been vastly amused."

"You are easily vastly amused. Isn't it Sext?"

"Well, you would have, too."

"What?"

"Well—thought Sex funny."

"Look here, mate," said Lucien, running his hands through his hanging hair and holding it upright, showing his curly mouth and fierce eyes, "I don't find sex funny."

Seb, a year younger, though a head taller and in the same form at school, felt his ignorance. "All right," he said.

"Sex is not funny." Lucien lay down flat on his back and closed his eyes.

Sebastian helped himself to several pea pods, scooping out and eating the peas, then chewing at the pods before spitting them at targets.

"I thought it was supposed to be all right."

"Huh!"

"Have you had an— Are you in a mess about something, then?"

Lucien didn't stir.

"In our house," said Seb, "there just didn't seem to be any sort of place for it." He ate more peas. "It was a pretty quiet life, really. My father was very quiet, you know, and one of my sisters and I, well, we're pretty, well, boring, I suppose. My mother's not boring. Nor's my younger sister. My mother's like a sort of engine. But you honestly can't imagine that my mother—well, that sex has ever even crossed her mind. Actually, my younger sister does discuss all sorts of—Freud and that sort of thing. But you don't listen to her."

"Why not?"

"Oh—she's a bit peculiar."

"Is she pretty?"

"No, she's hideous."

Lucien gave a tremendous sigh and sat up and also began picking peas. "Sex," he said.

Sebastian sat still, hoping. For a while there was no sound except for birds hopping in the pea sticks and the far-off noise of a tractor baling late hay.

"And of course you don't really meet anyone at school," Sebastian said.

"Don't you ever *go* anywhere?"

"No, not really. Father hates—hated going away. When you get back at end of term, anyway, you want to stay at home."

"*You* may."

"Why—what's wrong with yours, then?" (At school they were hardly acquaintances.)

"Nothing's right with it."

"What about your parents?"

"My mother went off. My father's always busy. He's manager of— Look, do you know who I spend my time with? Floozie waitresses, old ladies and shoe manufacturers."

"That's funny, my sister's spending her holidays with some shoe manufacturers. Freeman, Hardy and Willis."

"That's right, Freeman, Hardy and Willis."

"But what have Freeman, Hardy and Willis got to do with Sex?"

"Listen," said Lucien. "If you'd seen one fraction of the things I've seen: the absolute laziness and the squandor I've seen. Listen—in all the years I've been at that place—our great, palatial, glorified hotel—hotel de ville, hotel de vie—my God, in all the years I've lived there and I'm eighteen and I've been there since three—there's only one girl I've ever seen I'd give anything for at all."

89

"Well," said Seb, "I don't know that that's so funny. I've never met—"

Lucien lay down again.

"*Is* there such a word as squandor?" Seb asked presently.

"Listen," said Lucien, jerking up again, "this girl was beautiful. This girl was also all right. Not spoiled. I've seen millions who were good-looking, but I've never seen one who was also all right. So what do I do?"

"Well, you— I suppose you—"

"I don't. I didn't. That's what I'm telling you. I see this girl. The only girl I've ever— I see this girl and I never say one single word to her."

"Oh."

"I stand there like a great slob. What d'you think of that?"

"Well, I can understand—"

"First I meet her all alone. In the rain. Getting soaked. I'm in the dry. In a lonely empty shed in a wood. D'you know what I did?"

"Well, I—"

"I ran off. Yes. I ran off."

"Didn't you see her again?"

"Yes. I did. Needless to say, it would have to be when I'd got some floozie waitress hanging around."

"Well, why had you?"

"Oh, shut up. Then the last time it was a dance."

"Well, that should have been easy."

"Yes. Well. I dare say. There I was with the usual gathering who turn out for these things—twelve-year-olds, and old men with whiskers and check suits and buttonholes, and army officers' wives all teeth and diamond pins, and in she comes and sits down round the wall. With two old women. One's all right. A bit soft. The other's dreadful. Picks out everything.

90

She knows quite a bit about me, as a matter of fact. And this girl sat in between them looking terribly lonely. She had the most marvelous face. Really calm—as if nothing could ever spoil her, deep down. Terribly wise and good. Not silly, and—well, wonderful hair. So. What did I do?" he asked again.

"Well," said Seb. "Well—" He was beginning to find this astounding conversation oddly embarrassing. Lucien the Great! The world-weary Lucien! If anyone at school—! "Well, I suppose you asked her to dance."

"I didn't. I just looked at her. She saw me, too. I looked and looked at her and then I got hold of the nearest floozie and dragged her off onto the floor. I held her tight, too. Really tight. Didn't half give her a shock—she's one of Father's—and I danced up and down in front of her. This girl. It's a huge, great dance floor and there were hardly any people at the dance anyway. Why they have them, God knows. Melancholy isn't the word. Half a dozen couples dancing, half a dozen army officers and wives yacketing, Freeman, Hardy and Willis and all the kids fighting over the ping-pong table down the far end. *Spot* dances!"

"It does sound pretty fearful."

"It's fierce."

"It reminds me of something or someone," said Seb.

"Well, it's what I live in," said Lucien, "all the time except for school. That's why I joined you out here. Whatever it is, it's different."

"Yes, I like it here too," said Seb. "Who told you about it? Old Bell?"

"Yep."

"Me too."

"He's not so bad."

"No. Unstable a bit I'd think. Actually I got it wrong. I thought it was a Buddhist place."

"Probably Bell got it wrong. He's not all that accurate."

"As schoolmasters go, he is. He couldn't have thought it was Buddhist."

"Perhaps he thought you wouldn't come if you thought it was Christian since you'd had a lot of that at home."

"Oh, I don't think he's up to that."

"I don't know. He's a bit eccentric. Women go mad for him."

"Anyway, you're a Jew. What did he tell *you* about here?"

"I'm not a Jew. I'm Jew*ish*."

"Oh, ha-ha. Hilarious."

"Well, at least I knew where I was coming. Buddhist! You're as bad as the daisy on the phone."

A bell began to ring in the monastery behind them, a clear, delightful, innocent call.

"There's Sex," said Lucien, getting up and stretching. Smiling now too. "Oh, goodie goodie."

"Don't be silly, Sext is tomorrow now."

"Do you know something?" Lucien said. "I left the next day. I came for the six weeks here the next day. After the dance. I didn't see her again."

"You ought to tell old Father Ig about it."

"God! You couldn't tell him. Not this sex-obsession stuff."

"I expect you could," said Seb, suddenly bored. "I say, that female on the phone, thinking this was a Buddhist place like I did. I've just thought—"

"What?"

"I suppose it could have been one of my sisters."

Chapter Fourteen

Auntie Boo's school was really only one of the school houses, acquired later than the rest and separated from them by the two miles of drive Athene had just marched. The boys were carted in and out to the main school by bus—not the best arrangement but popular with those of a romantic turn of mind, for the house had been the Gothic mansion of a cotton king, quickly abandoned for something more orthodox and nearer Bolton.

It was a huge place, fit for an army with banners. The very front door stood forward in a stone box of pinnacles and cones and cried out for a drawbridge. Behind it arose high gray walls, battlements, turrets and curlicues, flagpoles, gingerbread chimneys and buttresses, finials, piers, plackets and buttresses, imitation stone lace, bowls, urns, jars, pedestals, ramparts, frets and goodness knows what. Athene had seen it all before, of course, some years ago at Sebastian's prize day, when they had stayed the night in the boys' sickroom, with Auntie Boo bellowing about with boxes of elastoplast and her mother saying, "How Boo shows off."

"But, my word, how I'd forgotten it," she thought now, looking down from the edge of the wood on the hill to where it stood, blissful and innocent and crazy as a castle in a book of tales, surrounded by green fields that the woods had drawn back from. Around its walls was even something of a moat in the pebbly beck that took a loop round it before making off down the meadows. The road she stood on dropped down and over this beck where white railings made a bridge.

She stopped there for a moment and looked up at the huge silent building, which looked back at her, mighty but not unfriendly. The vast front door was open a little and she walked in and called, "Auntie Boo."

There was no answer.

Overbright stained glass blazed at her from the curve of the staircase, which was black and very much beknobbed. Around the walls, green baize notice boards had been fixed onto the stone and the term's notices still curled up on them under drawing pins. A cricket bat lay on its back with string unwinding from its handle, and a box of gray garments, swept from under beds, had a paper arrow pointing down at it saying WHOSE ARE THESE? There was still the term-time smell of boys—apples on the turn—and utter silence. "Auntie Boo," she called again.

In the silence the coil continued. It would be so very odd not to know. About virginity. Well, it would be mad, really. Yet you can block things out. Immense things. Like the Polish airmen did who still worked on the farms round Westmorland. They'd blocked out all the tortures, Beams said.

And being born: you probably block that out. At least, you'd be sensible if you did. Beams said, Block out nothing. All

94

must be revealed, said Beams. But Beams was an awful ass.

Even Emily Brontë must have blocked out . . . You couldn't keep in your head all that happened to her and stay yourself.

So (face it) perhaps I blocked out Basil?

"I have blocked out Basil," she said to herself, and became aware that something was in fact blocking out her vision now, for where the banister crossed the stained glass there stood a man.

He was holding the banister and she could see only the top half of him, which was very tall and soared away into the air, sharp against the colored window as if he had been cut out of paper. He was a long, lean lamp-post of a man, or a queer, sideways, quizzical, mild bird of a man. He turned to face her and put both hands on the rail. Up went his shoulders and he brooded down over her—Mephistopheles, but delicate. A fine, spidery silhouette. The first primrose.

"I'm going mad," she thought.

"Good afternoon," she said and somewhere a telephone began to ring noisily. "I'm sorry," she said, "I'm Athene Price."

"Don't be sorry for that," said the silhouette.

"I mean I'm Matron's niece."

"Ah, yes. Well."

He came slowly down the stairs toward her. "I'm Henry Bell. How do you do? That is your aunt's telephone. It has been going all day and half the night. I can't get at it. It is her private one and locked in her flat. She's not here."

"But I was sure—"

"She's on a Red Cross affair. No one here but me and the telephone. One Bell to another. It is driving me mad. I am trying to mark papers."

The sun suddenly went behind the trees on the hills and the light went out of the window, leaving them alone in the cold hall.

"I didn't hear a car," he said.

"A *car?* Oh, no—I can't. I'm only . . . I walked."

"From the road? Dear me."

"Yes, I got a bus to the other end. I was coming to stay."

The telephone at last stopped.

"Well," he said. He stood thoughtfully examining the stone flags of the floor. There was an open fountain pen in one of his hands. The other took a sudden quick sweep round his hair, which stood up in peaks and spikes. It was red, and beneath it a curious, long face with a crooked nose and bright blue eyes, a khaki shirt, open at the neck, shorts and tennis shoes. Between shorts and shoes was an immense length of leg, but brown and sinewy, the hairs not noticeably the same color as on his head. He was very lean and narrow. As a piece of construction he was not excellent, but there was a sort of attraction about him.

"Hum," he said. "Oh, dear."

"Do you know when she's coming back?"

"I'm afraid not. The end of the week, I think. Perhaps next week."

"It's only Tuesday."

"Yes," he said. "A bad business. If you walk back to the road there's a bus into town again at seven. It's the last one. You might just catch it if you hurry. There are hotels and things."

"Yes," she said, "I see."

"I can't help much," he said. "I've no car either. Rather stuck out here. Getting these papers done. Only way."

"Yes, of course. Thank you very much," she said. "Good-bye."

"Goodbye," he said pleasantly. She went out and stood on the bridge and looked at the beck. Its bed was dry right across except in the middle, where polished brown water bubbled and turned over white stone eggs. She was cold about the legs under the night dress. There were four pounds in her purse.

She went back to the school and, since he had closed the door behind her, pulled a great iron chain with a ring at the end and waited.

There he was at once. He must still have been standing in the hall. Gold spectacles were now clipped to the end of the curious nose and he blinked over them amiably.

"Oh, hello."

She said, "I'm sorry. Could I just use your phone if you've got one? I'm in a bit of a spot. Especially if I miss the bus."

"Oh, yes," he said, "I hadn't thought of that." He fell over his tennis shoes rather as he shut the door. "I'm this way," he said, and led her up the staircases, through a stone door frame with a pointed arch and down a long passage covered with thin linoleum. A door toward the end of it stood open. "My phone's inside," he said, staying politely outside, looking out of the window at the long valley.

Inside, she stood looking at the telephone. She couldn't ring Sybil. Never. That was certain. She couldn't ring Posie; she had cadged enough. She couldn't ring Beams; she hadn't the number. She couldn't ring Seb—there wouldn't be a telephone in a monastery. She couldn't ring her mother—goodness knew where she was. The Isle of Wight? Richmond, Surrey? Timbuctoo?

She couldn't ring Boo—the Red Cross thing might be anywhere. But she had the feeling that there was someone she ought to ring. Somebody with some—well, some sense. "And whoever have I met lately with . . ." She pulled the phone toward her, picked up the phone book, searched about and dialed the operator.

"'ello," said Winnie's voice, "Cook's Cove Private Hotel."

"Oh. It's Athene Price. Miss Bowles'—"

"Ah."

"I just thought I'd better ring."

"That's right."

"Just to tell them—Miss Bowles—to let them know—not to worry. I've got here."

"That's right."

"To my aunt's. Thank you very much."

"That's right. They're in a right taking."

"I'm sorry."

" 'ere, d'you want anything?"

(What do I want?)

"No, thanks, I'm quite all right. Could you say I'm, sorry—er—about the pixie hood."

"It's brought back. And he carried back the luggage."

"Oh?"

"Any address? They're in a two-and-eight. 'ello? 'ello? Are you there?" she went on after a pause. " 'ere, is there any messages?"

Athene put down the phone and one and sixpence on the phone book, adding a second shilling in case it wasn't six o'clock. She sat on at the odd man's desk, looking at it. A nice desk. A nice room. Flowers in pots, books all over the walls, a big window looking down the valley, the wandering beck angling its way out of sight. A still evening.

All over the desk were exam papers with marks on them in a very firm black hand, the final percentage thick and bold at the top of each page 1. Two lots of marking. This man must be the final examiner. "No. 384," she read. "The general having

deposited all his troops in Carthage proceeded to harass—"
Then the pen in a vehement black line. Surprising. He had
such thin fingers.

"The general having positioned all his forces—" (No. 385,
the last one finished. 72%. A good one) "—near Carthage,
proceeded—" There were huge heaps still to do, great postal
packages all over the floor. She was being a nuisance.

She put her head out of the door and said, "I'm terribly
sorry. I have phoned someone, but I don't think—I don't know
that it'll help. There's no one who can—"

"Oh, dear," he said.

"I'm dreadfully sorry to interrupt you, but isn't there any
way of getting into Auntie Boo's flat?"

"I don't think so."

"But—I mean, there must be. What if there was a fire or
something?"

He looked alarmed. "Good heavens! I hadn't thought of it."

"Well, I mean, it's unlike her. Isn't there a caretaker?"

"Not whilst I'm here. He is on holiday. It is a problem."

"I suppose," she said, "I suppose I couldn't just stay here
somewhere?" (Basil? Nonsense. Another world.)

He turned distant blue eyes on her and said, "Only the
dormitories. You could stay in a dormitory. There are blankets
still, I think. No sheets, of course."

"That wouldn't matter."

He looked longingly at his desk. "Then that's all right,
then," and, nodding to her, he sat down.

"Shall I go and find one? A dormitory?"

"There are plenty," he said. "Five or six."

"My brother's here. Sebastian Price."

"Oh, good," he said. "You could find his bed perhaps."

"And what about food?" she thought. "And a toothbrush?

And a comb? And clothes, come to that?" She found a dormitory and made up the far-end bed with blankets. Then she went downstairs looking for the kitchens, but what looked like the door to the kitchens was locked. She went back to the hall and began to sort through the gray garments. There was a pair of flannel cricket trousers at the bottom and a clean and folded blue games jersey. There were also many socks. Her feet were freezing, but she could not somehow cope with the socks. There are limits.

There was a cleanish-looking bath towel too, and on a lonely landing she found a bathroom with three baths in a row and a transparent oval of soap. She tried the water, which seemed miraculously to be boiling, locked the door, bathed and put on her nightdress and mackintosh again.

In the dormitory she laid out the cricket flannels and jersey for morning, opened the uncurtained window a little and got into the blanketed bed. It was not eight o'clock.

There was an uncertain noise at the door. "I just thought of food," said the vague voice.

"It's all right," she said, "I had some on the way. At a bus station."

He did not reply and after a long time she said into the yellowish ticking of the pillow, "I'm far past eating anyhow."

But there was a crash of falling forks and he tapped again and said, "I say, hello. There are eggs," and she took her face out of the pillow and saw that it was morning.

"Yes?" she called.

"I've scrambled some eggs," he said. "And there's a letter."

Putting on her mac, she walked the long mile of wood to the door. He stood with a tray, holding it loosely as if someone else

100

had thrust it into his hands. "It is ten," he said. "I thought you might be ill."

"Oh, no—I must have been tired. I'm terribly hungry."

"There, then. The letter is 'to await arrival.' "

"Well, I do seem to have. Arrived," she said, for he was looking very steadily at her. "Not exactly with me," she thought, then noticed a toothbrush in a cellophane packet on the tray beside the eggs and coffee.

"Oh, heavens! Oh, how kind. My luggage isn't—isn't here yet. How many papers did you finish?" She smiled wider—the particular smile of the summerhouse and Basil's cottage after the kippers.

But Henry Bell looked away. "Not enough," he said. "I must get back to some more. Excuse me."

Chapter Fifteen

The Bishop's Palace,
Pimlico, S.W.1

Dearest,

A quick word. A really quick word for I am catching a train
to Lancashire. I have *much to tell* you, darling. A most amazing
thing has been suggested for us. I can't of course make a
decision before I have put it to you all. It will not be
long—next week. I will phone you at Boo's telling Boo exactly
when I want her to drive you over to Darlington to meet me. I
will also contact Beams' people who must now be back in
Tadcaster (?) and Sebastian's chief monk. Perhaps you won't
be with her very long—things are moving so fast.

I am now going to Manchester. There is little point
probably but Mabel Palethorpe has been so kind in making all
the arrangements (Housekeeper. Women's hall of residence in
University. Big flat. Room for us all. But *Manchester!*) and I

am staying a few days with her because she is so frail. She was only a bag of bones last time and that was three years ago. She doesn't eat. I am buying her some fish at the Army and Navy Stores—smoked haddock—which she will be able to digest. Last time it was nothing but bakewell tart and china tea and a bad egg. I had to put the inside into an *envelope,* leaving the shell on the breakfast tray. So difficult.

As you see I am now in London. Pimlico is hopeless. She runs the diocese. He is a nice old thing with fat lips—just sits all day in his study and she tells him what comes next. God help the Church. That horrible Priscilla does social work for the Fabian Society and breast-feeds at the table—looks like a rag bag. Mother of course still has very good clothes and the curtains are thick green brocade. Talks all the time about the theater and who is coming to dinner. *Somehow* they get meat. I suggested they give it away to the poor now that rations are so small and she gave me one of those awful stares.

Well, darling, I hope you had a lovely time with Posie and lots of fun with Sybil—swimming and sunbathing, with any luck. I believe the friend she lives with is a *real* character.

Tell me all next week.

Much love from Mother.

P.S. If you and Boo could stop at that shop near Darlington station and get one of those apple pies—a plate-cake—and some eccles cakes. That would take care of tea if we can't go on to Scarborough (I'll explain later). You will be astounded at where we may be having tea!! A secret. Lots of love, M.

Athene read the letter on the terrace at the top of some mossy steps between stone urns, and stood for some time afterward looking at the view. Sighing, in the end she stretched up and dropped it into one of the urns and turned back toward the house. Her whole mind turned away from the letter. To help it she examined all the ranks of windows, the clusters of chimneys, the flowers blazing in the borders, the crimson creeper on the wall, its first few dead leaves scratching their claws on the terrace stones in the breeze.

Nothing to do, she thought. No chair, no book, not even any sewing. No one to talk to. Nowhere to go.

Well, she might go for a walk. She might walk down the valley to the end of the beck. She might walk down the woods again and catch a bus to the town and buy toothpaste and bread and so on. She set off along the flagstone path, along the back of the house, under the one open window above her head. The smell of pipe smoke floated down. She deliberately walked faster, briskly, not looking up. No one with such a step could be thought a lingerer. No head would look out, hearing such a determined passer-by.

No head did.

Three hours later she was striding back, down the valley this time, which looked as if it might be rather quicker than the woods. She followed the path of the beck, zigzagging nearer and nearer, looking carefully at the stones, sometimes jumping over them. At the end of the valley stood the house. The huge study window on its flank looked at her. Whenever she raised her eyes she looked intently at the view to either side of it.

When she was under the window again a head did look out. He blinked at her, took off his glasses and said, "I've made some curry. Would you care for lunch?" He smiled. She thought, "How strange, he's quite good-looking."

"I'd love some."

He took a quick sweep round his hair again, leaving ink on his face. "You look well," he said.

"I've been for a walk."

The head disappeared, but then shot out again. "If I had plaits," he said, "I could be Rapunzel in reverse."

Well, I never, she thought. That was a joke.

He reminds me of someone, she thought, washing up the dishes. She hung up the tea towel in his flat kitchen and went back to the study.

He was opening another batch of papers.

"Would you like—?"

"Hmmm?"

"Coffee?"

"Oh, yes," he said. "Nice."

"You're well stocked up here," she called through as she lit the kettle. "I bought some bread this morning."

"Bread calls," he said. "In a van. And milk."

"Do you cook for yourself in term time?"

"Good heavens, no. I don't live here in the term."

"Don't you?"

"No, thank you."

She came in with the coffee. It seemed rude to ask, Where do you live?

"Do you live in one of the other houses?"

"Any sugar?"

"Oh—sorry."

She sat on the window seat drinking her coffee. The sun was more gold than it had been. August nearly over.

"It's not an earthly paradise," he said.

"What?"

"It's not an earthly paradise here, you know. Just a convenient pitch for getting a job done."

"It *seems* an earthly paradise." Red leaves framed the window. The sky behind was clear and blue and high.

"Well, perhaps," he said, clipping on the glasses, pulling forward papers, looking sideways at her once, quickly.

"Yes—but look at it," she said. As he did not, she sat on and found herself reading the top page of a finished package of papers on the window seat beside her.

"I suppose it is 'harassed,'" she said thoughtfully.

"What?"

"I suppose 'harassed' is right?"

"It'd better be after I've marked a thousand papers."

"It's a rotten word, though, isn't it? Not strong enough. Somehow it reminds me of my mother."

He said, slashing with his pen, "You do Latin?"

"Yes. I did."

"Any Greek?"

"Yes."

"Well, that's good."

"I don't know. I'm doing Chemistry, really."

A pause. "You're bright, then? Clever?" He suddenly heaved himself up and grabbed the milk jug and began pouring a lot of milk into his coffee, stirring it all about. "As well as beautiful."

She gave the most enormous jump and her saucer rattled.

"Mind the papers," he said.

In the end she said, "I don't know whether I'm really very clever. You couldn't really feel clever in our house with someone as good as—my father—about."

Something had changed in the room. There was now no necessity for her to leave him alone, nor likelihood that he would dismiss her. He went on with his work, apparently unaware of her. She leaned her head against the window frame in the hot, quiet afternoon.

106

"Athene." It was another study and raining.

"Athene, are you busy?"

"Not a bit. Why?"

He put his long fingers over his face and then stretched long arms and yawned.

"You'll tear your cassock."

"Shall we go for a walk?"

"It's pouring."

"I know. But I want to walk."

"It's raining cats and dogs."

"I know. But I want a walk. Shall we go up the moor?"

"Mother would go mad. You'd get your death."

"Worth it. Got to die sometime."

"Father, for heaven's sake."

"Exactly. It's getting empty."

"But it's pouring. Wait till it stops and we'll go in the garden or something. We ought to do the raspberries."

"Bother the raspberries. Be a good girl and find my galoshes."

"All right, but you'll need a sou'wester and so will I."

"You're a good, kind girl."

The valley dissolved before her as she sat looking at it with the coffee cup in her lap. When it returned into focus nothing had changed. He sat on, Henry Bell, with his back to her, absorbed and still. How hot it was—thunder seemed to be rumbling about in the distance. How still the flowers stood outside, and how stiff and listening on the window ledges.

"Be a nice, kind girl," he said.

In a daze she got off the window seat.

"Do up some papers for me. Shove them into packets. Check them over."

She knelt on the floor and began, at first slowly and then more briskly. They were in no muddle and only needed collecting.

"Shall I do the labels? Stick them on?"

"Yes, please." He worked on. She stacked them up, waited for more, saw they were in the right order, piled them in boxes. Sometimes there was nothing to do while she waited for the end of a batch. She sat on the floor, idle, sleepy. At about five she made tea and he looked up. "Not much more now. You are a good girl." She wandered away.

She went off down the passage, down the baronial staircase, touching the telephone that stood on the landing as she passed, in the hall looking at but not reading the notices on the boards. She opened a door and found a music room, a grand piano very battered near the window. It was stifling hot.

She opened the piano, then the window, and stood with her fingers on the rounded keys. It wasn't a bad piano. She played something. Thunder flapped far off. She sat down and played some more. No breath stirred in the room nor outside, not a breath in the trees, not a petal moved. She hit a note and said as it died away, "It is not going out, it is here forever. There is no time. It is enchanted here." She got up and went out onto the terrace, waiting for him. But he did not come.

PART THREE

September

Chapter Sixteen

Father Ignatius knew exactly what to expect. He knew the moment he heard the knock and Sebastian's pleasant face came round the door. "Yes, of course," he said, trying not to sigh at the predictability of things. "I'm nearly eighty," he thought. "How many generations of men have I had to tell they are mistaken?"

"I just wanted to ask you, Father . . ."

He pulled a blotter forward on his desk, closed his eyes quickly, asking for strength, and said, "Of course, Sebastian. I hope nothing's wrong?" and waited for the usual tentative inquiry. The monastic life, the chance of being considered—how one can know? He had the usual answers ready; the usual deterrents. At eighteen one cannot know. Only once or twice in a lifetime had he met a man with an unquestionable vocation. And if he, Sebastian, were in doubt of any kind, then he had not one. Etc., etc. "Come in, Seb. Sit down. What's the question?"

"Well, it's not a question, really," said Seb. "It's just a fact. I just thought I'd better ask you what I could do about it since I haven't any money for the phone."

"Oh," said Father Ignatius, hastily readjusting his thoughts. "Phone?"

"I'm worried about my sister. I've a very strong feeling she is trying to get in touch with me."

"Dear me—I hope you're not becoming a spiritualist."

"Oh, no," said Seb, "she's not dead. It was my father—"

"Yes, of course. I'm sorry."

"There's no need to be sorry," said Seb and sat like a rock.

"You say that your sister . . ." prompted Father Ignatius at length.

Seb said, staring at the wall behind the father's head, "Also it was about sin."

"Yes?" said Father Ignatius, startled. "Sin?"

"I very much detested my father," said Seb conversationally. "He died in July and I am very glad he did."

"I see."

"I imagine, however, that this is a sin. I want to know what to do about being glad about it."

"I see." Father Ignatius looked under his swirling white eyebrows that needed a tonsure much more than his head. "Perhaps you should tell me more about your reasons."

"Well, he was just ghastly," said Seb equably. "He was just someone I couldn't stand. And yet—the queer thing was I was absolutely alone in thinking so. Everyone adored him. Women anyway. He was mad about women."

Father Ignatius said, "I think this is not my department."

"But he was. Oh, not like that. Old women. Old pussycats. Our house was full of them. They all doted on him, closeted up with him for hours and Mother absolutely working herself to death. She did all the floors in our rectory—and if you saw

112

it, you'd know. She did about what six brothers do in this monastery, and all the cooking and shopping and organizing and flowers and Mothers' Union and Young Wives and vestments and bazaars and Missions to Seamen and entertaining all the wretched bishops who were always landing—water jugs in the bedrooms, finger bowls if it was old York."

"My dear Seb—"

"And he was absolutely taken up with my sisters. Well, I know they had a worrying time with Beams, my younger one—she was a bit dotty when she was young. Mind you, she'd have been all right, it always seemed to me, if they'd just left her alone—carting her off to concerts in her pram, thinking she was a genius, saying Beethoven couldn't read or something. But my elder sister, Athene, well, he absolutely ate her alive. Greek and stuff at five. Long heart-to-hearts all over the moors. Roaming about with his hair flowing, in a great black hat and cloak like Tennyson or something. You'd have thought Athene was Charlotte Brontë or something, the way he absolutely cherished her."

"And what about you?"

"Oh, he hardly noticed me. I was a sort of lay figure. He was just mad on women. It wasn't particularly attractive, you know, a man of that age."

"I'm sorry."

"Well, he was pretty old when—when we were all born. My mother's much younger. It—well, it makes you feel rather ill."

Father Ignatius looked down at the blotter. "And so you want to know—?"

"Oh, I just want to know if it's a sin—something you can't change—not loving him. And also I was thinking, could I possibly be allowed to ring my sister?"

113

Looking at the bland face, Father Ignatius thought how much here ought to be broken down for safety, and wondered if ever it would be. Not in the two days more he was to stay. He also felt suddenly immensely old.

"Which sister?" he asked.

"Athene."

"The pagan sister? How beautiful they were—the pagan names."

"That's what Father thought," said Seb levelly.

"Look—" Father Ignatius leaned forward over his hands— "I really know very little about young girls. We don't see many. Maybe we ought to see more." He cackled. "Just as well you're not the press. Tell me why you think you should get hold of this Athene."

"Well, I think she rang me. Lucien was on reception and there was a girl asking for a Buddhist monastery—"

"You did say it was the *younger* sister who was peculiar?"

"Yes." For the first time Sebastian looked ill at ease. "Actually, I think maybe I gave them the idea."

"Really?" The rolling eyebrows shot up.

"My younger sister wouldn't ring up. She's pretty self-possessed."

"The one who is like Beethoven?"

"Yes," said Seb. "There's not much bothers her."

"*I* see. Do you know where your elder sister is?"

"Well, yes, I think so. I think she's with our aunt at my school—my aunt's the Matron. We're scattered a bit since Father died. Mother's trying to find us somewhere to live. Father kept on taking no thought for the morrow, knowing she'd manage when she had to, even without a bean. Which she will. She's very brave, my mother. Everyone thinks she's belligerent and dreadful—but she's fantastically brave. She's in

114

the Isle of Wight trying to find lodgings or something. My other sister's with friends."

"You know, Sebastian," said Father Ignatius. "I really know very little about the safekeeping of females, as I say, but I simply cannot think of anywhere better for your elder sister—safer, securer—than in a school empty of boys in charge of the Matron."

"No—I suppose not."

"I think, you know, you are worrying quite unnecessarily. If anything were wrong I feel sure I should hear of it. The point of these Retreats, you know, is that you get rid of your home ties and day-to-day anxieties. This is why we say no letters or phone calls."

"Yes, I know," said Seb. "Actually, though, I did ring."

"Oh, you did."

"Yes. I rang last night. From the hall phone when no one was about. I'm sorry."

"I see. And what happened?"

"Well, that's what's so funny. I rang really quite late—it's miles in the country. She wouldn't be out. But there wasn't a reply."

"You rang your aunt's number?"

"Yes."

"And there really is no one else who knows where your sister is?"

"Well, there's two sort of women of Father's who were supposed to be having her. I"—he looked at his hands—"I did actually ring them, too, and one said she'd gone to the other's, and when I rang the other there was a sort of drunk-sounding woman on the other end who said Athie had gone to our aunt's."

"I am surprised," said Father Ignatius, holding his head,

"that after this telephoning you did not try your aunt's once more."

"Well, that's it," said Seb. "I had no money left. We had to hand it over when we got here."

"So I was thinking."

"Well, I did find a bit somewhere for the other calls. I put it in the box."

"And you now want more?"

"Well, yes, I do."

"Oh—go away," said Father Ignatius suddenly. "Go away. I'll think about it." As Seb went off he covered his face and thought, not for the first time, how lucky he was to be a monk. He thought of his own sister and found it difficult to recall her face. "Which is as it should be," he thought, and walked to the window. "For me, though. Not for that one." He rang a bell and a novice arrived. "Give Sebastian this," he said, handing over some coins. "Tell him to use the phone box outside the gates, and that he can have three minutes only. Then tell him to make an appointment to see me on the other matter. And tell him he's going home early. I've had a note from his mother this morning."

Chapter Seventeen

Athene was dreaming she was in the bath and couldn't turn the taps off. The shower was on above her head too—it was the great big bathroom at Crag Foot. Auntie Posie was standing in the bathroom doorway in a lacy garment, eating cake. The water thundered down: she gasped and struggled to get to the taps. Waking, she found she was in the dormitory. It was the middle of the night, outside the rain crashed down in torrents and Henry Bell stood at her bedroom window in his pajamas, looking out.

In spite of the noise of the storm, he seemed to know she had woken because he said, without turning, "I'm trying to shut your window."

She sat up in bed and pulled the gray blanket up to her chin. Lightning lit up the long room and almost before it was gone came the thunder. "Hell," he said, ducking inward from the window. There was more lightning, an immense thunderclap and the rain splattered down like hoses. "Are you all right?" he asked, standing in the window bay, still not looking round.

"Yes."

"I thought you might be afraid."

"No. I love storms."

"In fact, you were asleep."

"Yes."

"I'm sorry."

There was more thunder, two great forks of lightning photographing the high line of woods; then again the rain.

"It's very hot," he said, turning at last toward her as she sat in the pyramid of the blanket. "It's a funny thing—have you noticed that thunder never really clears the air?"

She said in a cold, rather formal voice that seemed new to her, "Did you finish?"

"Yes. Just. I finished the last one to the sound of trumpets."

"There's been an awful lot of thunder this summer," she said in the same strange voice.

He came over and stood at the end of her bed. "Talking about the weather," he said.

To her surprise, she said, "My father's dead."

"Yes," he said, "I know."

"You *know?*"

"Yes."

"How could you know?"

"I knew Price's father died at the end of last term. He went home for the funeral."

"Well, go on," she said in a minute, bitterly. "Go on."

"With what?" There was another clap of thunder, and rain was splashed into the room by the wind. "That window," he said, and went back and leaned out to it again.

"Tell me how old you heard he was. Gaga, etc."

118

Slamming the window, he shook wet arms, turned and leaned against it. "How old are you?" he said.

"Seventeen—well, in September."

"Now, in fact."

"No, not yet. On the second. It's still August."

"It's September. I know. The papers had to be done by the first. They were done today. You're seventeen tomorrow."

"It can't be. Well—there'd have been cards and things."

For a moment she thought he was going to come across to her. Instead he turned quickly round toward the night. "It strikes me there probably are some cards—post galore, and that phone of your aunt's rampaging. I expect it was all for you. Perhaps you don't open letters?"

"I did the one you brought up," she said. "I haven't looked for any more." She had been with him now two full days.

He stretched an arm out sideways as he looked intently at the darkness and said, "Come over here and look."

She got slowly out of bed, clutching the blanket, and went and stood beside him about three feet away. There was not much to see—white foam wild in the beck, a faint outline of the urn where her mother's letter presumably floated. Not a light for miles. The great, dark house empty all round them.

"Tomorrow," he said, "shall we go out somewhere?"

"No," she said fiercely. "*No.*"

"Yes," he said. "Yes. Tomorrow we are going out somewhere. For your birthday."

"I don't want my birthday. I just want to be here. Just like this."

"Like this?" he said. Looking quickly at him, sideways, she saw the amused, long face laughing at her. He lifted an arm and took up a handful of her long hair. "Athene," he said.

At about the same moment the telephone began to ring.

119

"Don't answer it," he said. "I'm not going to."

"You must," she said. "It's terribly late. It might be important."

He said, holding her hair, "It's only about eleven. You go early to bed. And always without saying good night."

"But it's not the usual phone. It's not yours or Auntie Boo's either. It's the one on the landing—the school one."

"Is one phone more important than another? Or less important?"

"Well—it might be for— Look, please answer it."

"I thought you wanted to be just here—like this."

"I'll answer it."

"Do as you please," he said, tossing her hair away from him. She flew out onto the landing and heard Seb's laconic voice say, "Oh, hello. It is you, is it? I thought I'd try the caretaker's number. I was just going to ring off."

Chapter Eighteen

The next morning she stood in Skipton marketplace, or rather on the steps of Skipton Public Library, in a new dress she had bought at one of the stalls. It was a white dress, silky and shiny and covered with orange and black whirls and streaks. It had a V neck and had cost two pounds. From another stall she had bought some white sandals, though not stockings; a shampoo sachet to be mixed with water that evening; a Tangee lipstick, 1s. 3d. She had carried her parcels to the public library, where she had changed in the W.C.s, dumping the cricket flannels and shirt in a wastepaper basket, and she appeared outside the library like a harvest moon.

The dress of course must have been rayon, but the stars in their courses had inspired the design on it. It was the dress of a lifetime. The people of Skipton noticed it, and her bright eyes. Henry, who had been buying bus tickets, waited for her to come up to him and said, "Many happy again returns."

"Do you like it? I wish I'd bought it before lunch."

"Why?"

"Well, then I could have worn it."

"I liked the other ensemble. Though on anyone else, I may say . . ." He got hold of her arm.

She thought, I am absolutely happy with him. I know all the things to say. Everything I say is all right. People looked at them as they walked close together across the square. "Oh, dear," she said as they got near the bus, "Is it a tour?"

"No," he said, "just the usual Brontë bus. It goes on until October."

"*What* bus?"

"The Brontë bus. To Haworth. It's the local showplace. You're going, my girl, whether you like it or not. Even if you've been a dozen times."

"I haven't. Not ever."

"Neither have I." They queued up.

People were standing in groups about the bus and some already getting into it, keeping seats for each other, examining guidebooks.

"Does it go every day?" she asked.

"I suppose so."

"And not from here only?"

"Oh, no—from Harrogate, York and Leeds and Scarborough, I suppose. They come from London, Americans, and back for supper. From Rome, Tibet, Afghanistan. Hurrah for the three weird sisters."

"*Every* day?"

"Well—a lot of days. Only twice a week from Tibet."

They waited until most of the people had assorted themselves inside. "What is it?" he asked. "What is it, Athene?"

"Oh, nothing."

122

"What is it?"

"Oh, I was just thinking. They were so alone. That was really the whole point."

"Yoo-hoo," came out of the bus and a fat lady in a knitted suit tried to wind down a window and flap a handkerchief. A cross person behind jabbed her shoulder, saying, "I can't stand draft." "I can stand any amount of wind," he told his friends, "but I can't stand draft."

It was some sort of party that filled the whole of the downstairs of the bus, so they went upstairs and sat at the front in the seats that hang out over the driver. They bounced about and two ladies parallel, overspill from downstairs, screamed with joy as they reverberated through Airedale.

"Who are they all?" she asked in a whisper.

"An Outing."

"But *why*—?"

"I don't know. The Brontës were—"

"Oh, yes—but why *these* people?"

"I like them," he said gently, finding her hand. "I like their nice faces and pearls and fur-felt hats and permanent waves."

She sat still.

"And their ornaments. The claws of their tam o'shanters and fishbone brooches."

"Aren't you being a bit—" She stopped. She felt the least breath of unease, then great regret for it. Could this end after all? Enchantments do fade. Then disbelief. No, not this. Not ever.

"Aren't you being a bit, well, patronizing?"

He examined her fingernails one at a time and said, "Who do you think they all are?"

"I don't know. An Outing. Who?"

"North country novelists," he said.

"Henry! Some of them are men."

"Well, some of them *are* men."

"Don't you like north country novelists?"

"Ain't no sich things," he said. "Not even the Brontës. Look, we're in Keighley."

Airedale opened and spread before them, rose and fell. Stone walls climbed precipices, fells and heather stretched blue and faint. A main road at last, a roundabout, an ugly railway station, a car-park.

"This is an awful place," said Athene. "It can't be—"

"It is."

"Oh, no! Look, you can see other places, other villages on the hills. It's not moors."

"What were you expecting? Bodmin?"

"I don't know anything about Bodmin."

"It's such a color," she said as they began to walk up the steep main street. The Outing was gathering itself together, busy with powder puffs around the station waiting room. "It's *purple*. It's a purple, ugly place. Like a mining town."

"What's wrong with purple?" Henry led her to the side of the street. Looking at her, he said, "My word, you mind! You are a morbid child—you wanted all wilderness and desolation."

"No," she said.

"Look at this and cheer up." He pointed to a notice pasted on a wall.

The MERRY MIDGETS
This STUPENDOUS COMPANY
of DWARFS AND JUGGLERS
are to visit
HAWORTH
on Saturday, September 17th

124

"Dwarfs and jugglers," he said.

"For Branwell," she said. They smiled.

"Well, not for Emily or Charlotte or the old boy."

She laughed and they went on, climbing up the cobbles, slowly because of all the people, passing the Branwell Café, the Heathcliff Heights. The sound of the hatted ladies behind grew nearer—the Outing catching up.

"Perhaps for Emily," she said, "and yes, I think for Anne. In fact, they'd all have gone."

"You sound an authority." He swirled his hair about in his usual way. He looked very happy. They turned left at the top of the cobbled street, passed the church to the parsonage.

Inside they stood close together in the sitting room and were told that here the girls had sat and worked. "And there," pointed the gaunt guide, "is the sofa on which Emily died." Athene looked at it intently and thought, "He is looking at me."

"Not unlike your mother's," said someone behind.

"Well, it's the spit of Dolly's," said a man.

Across the passage was the stern room where Mr. Brontë had eaten twenty years alone.

"Well, he was funny," said a voice.

"*You'd* get funny, living all this way," said another.

There was a commotion as the bus party reached the front door and a pause while they bought their tickets. The guide directed the rest to wait.

"This is the sofa on which Emily died."

"Look, Alice, isn't it like Auntie's?"

Up the stairs, straight ahead was the little room that had been Emily's with a red rope across the doorway. Athene altered course and went off to the right. *Charlotte's Room* said a ticket on the door, and there was her London dress, all little

125

flowers under a glass case—a rusty bonnet, some tired gloves. "My, she were little—look, Dorothy."

"Well, they'd nowt to eat. He kept them starving."

"They were all little then. Look at Henry the Eighth."

"I wouldn't call Henry the Eighth little."

"Well, short, then."

("He is looking at me.")

"Henry the Eighth was before."

"Well, not a lot, was it?"

She walked across to the case and, examining every fold of the neat, determined little dress, the balding brown velvet collar, saw none of it. She thought, "He is looking at me all the time."

"You couldn't call them Elizabethans. They were around Dickens."

He touched her wrist and said, "Come and see Emily's room."

"No, it's all right."

"What's the matter? Come on." They stood side by side in the doorway. "How small," he said. "Funny, I'd have thought it would be at the back of the house looking at the moors. Not over that fearful graveyard. My God, look at those trees— they're tipping up the very dead."

"Yes."

A voice from across the landing—Branwell's room, where he had shrieked and fallen drunk and set fire to the bed curtains—was saying that Branwell hadn't been much of a painter.

"He pouted everybody's mouth out. Maybe he couldn't see straight. They probably didn't look like that at all."

"Look at that queer ostrich one with the neck. That'll be Emily."

"Mind, Anne was the only pretty one. And insipid, rather."

Through Emily's window, the window where she had gazed through the night at the moon and been one with God, another troupe of tourists could be seen approaching, surging into the hall below, and their own busload was squashed up on the landing behind them. Athene was pushed against Henry. There were cries and laughs. She was touching him all down his side, from his shoulder to his ankle. He put his arm round her and held on to her tightly. "I suppose you know that I have fallen in love with you," he said.

"This way," called the guide, "Needlework Guild this way. Move up now, please," and one of the ladies of the bus party detached herself and buffeted through the crowd toward their backs. "Yes," she said, "I knew it was. It's Henry Bell! Well—to think that you and Pattie have a girl as big as this already." Then she looked alert and sharply and said, "But goodness me!" and Athene turning round saw Mrs. Messenger.

Chapter Nineteen

When the bus stopped at the school stop he snapped his book shut and sprang out and was over the road and striding to the gates of the school drive without a glance at her. She had to hurry after. There had not been seats together on the bus. She had had to sit at the front among squirming children. He had been at the back on one of the sideways seats over the wheel, reading intently what looked like some textbook whenever she looked round.

She caught up with him at the gate, which he was unfastening. He looked proud and distant and was wearing his glasses. Not looking at her, he said, "What happened to the cricket flannels?"

"I—I— *What!!*"

"You seem to have disposed of the cricket flannels."

"I dumped them in Skipton library."

"I suppose you know that they are school property."

"*What!*" She stood astounded.

He flung away, loping ahead through the trees and round a bend out of sight. She must have stood there for minutes before she called out "Henry!" and began to run after him.

"Henry!" she cried as he came into sight again. How fast he walked. She began to run again and her hair came loose and fell about her face. "Henry," she called, "oh, Henry, Henry." He went even faster and, stumbling over a tree root, she stopped and covered her face and thought, "I am Athene Price. I am running and calling after a man who must be nearly thirty and is married and does not want me." Again Henry disappeared around a bend and, closing her eyes and swallowing hard, she composed her face and said out loud, "I am Athene Price. Soon I will be a Scholar of Lady Margaret Hall. I am seventeen today. I intend to become a scientist." Then she went on more slowly and with some grace, tying back her hair as she walked, taking a handkerchief from her pocket and rubbing the palms of her hands. "I am Athene Price. My father was a saint and Rural Dean. I have a deep understanding of the work of Emily Brontë."

But round the next corner all was as nought, for he was standing stock still in the middle of the path waiting for her to catch up with him, looking far into the distance.

She came up to him and walked round him—and she had the sudden outrageous notion that she might almost laugh. She turned to face him and they stood there for a while as it grew dark. She said in the end, "How long have you been married?"

"Ten years."

"Have you any children?"

"Two."

"Where are they?"

"In France. She's French."

"Is she—"

"What?"

"Is she pretty?"

"Oh, Athene." He closed his eyes.

"How could you?"

"I meant it."

"How could you!"

"What I said. Before she—that woman—"

"I don't mean that."

"What do you mean?"

"About the cricket flannels."

He opened his eyes and said, "Well, I was trying. Trying to get things right."

"Right! It was a terrible thing to say. It was the cruelest thing to say you could have thought of."

"It was a quick way of stopping it. Athene, I'm thirty-four. You are alone with me in the school. I teach your brother. And my God, girl, I'm married."

"You didn't think that last night."

"What?"

"When you didn't want me to answer the phone."

"I went away," he said. "After the phone."

"It doesn't matter."

"Athene."

"Nothing matters." Lady Margaret Hall forgotten, she cried, "Nothing matters."

"Look, dear," he said uneasily and put out a hand.

She flung it away. "Oh, *stop* that," she said. "Don't be so dishonest. It's the same for me. Don't you see, it's the same for me?

"I love you, too," she said. "You fool, you know it's so. How *can* you!" She turned away, leaning her head on a branch. "Oh Henry, Henry, how can you let that evil woman—"

"It wasn't that."

"Yes, it was. You know it was. It was in Emily's room. You knew it there, too. We both knew it and then that—devil came. And then—oh, Henry—the cricket flannels!"

He made a sort of helpless, gulping, laughing noise and went over to her.

She turned. "You know it's true. We must stay together. I must stay with you forever."

He said slowly, "I have never seen any one so—" and stopped. "Don't cry," he said.

"I never cry." She clung to him.

After a time he put his arm round her and said, "All right. All right, Athene, I'm sorry. All right. Oh, Athene—come home," and they walked out of the wood.

But alas, below them the school was a blaze of lights, and Auntie Boo patrolled the terrace.

Chapter Twenty

"If I give up my ticket now," said Mrs. Price to the ticket collector on Darlington station, "do you suppose I might be allowed back?"

"Back?" said the ticket collector, examining his punching machine.

"Back," said Mrs. Price. "Onto the platform again. This afternoon is going to be most difficult to organize. Many threads are about to be gathered up."

"That's right," said the man. (You meet all sorts.)

"So I may?"

"What?"

"Come back?"

"If you buy a platform ticket you can come back."

"Oh, good gracious," said Mrs. Price, "what nonsense. Then I shall stay this side until the Edinburgh express comes in."

"That's right," said the man.

"I have just alighted from the *London* express," she added.

132

"That's right."

"And I intend to meet my son, who has been staying in a Buddhist monastery, from the *Edinburgh* express."

"You do that," said the man, easing little bits of ticket out of the hole; but his opposite number, in the upright box on the other side of the barrier, suddenly called out, "Platform One."

"I beg your pardon?"

"Queen of Scots coming, Platform One," he said.

"*Thank* you," said Mrs. Price, giving a triumphant look at the first man, "that is exactly what I wanted to know. Perhaps you would both be good enough to look out for several people who should be arriving in a moment and asking for me. There will be a chauffeur—Miss Dixon's chauffeur—and a Dr. Padshaw and a Miss Bowles, and also—"

"Queen of Scots coming," said the official. "Best move across now."

"Keep them," said Mrs. Price, raising an admonishing arm, "at all costs," and moved toward the platform.

"She'll be an actress, likely," said the first man as the train roared in, filling the station with smoke.

Seb jumped out with his pack swinging, and Lucien's head appeared at a window. "This is Lucien," Seb said to his mother. "He's been with me. He's going on."

"Well, but how nice," she said. "I'd no idea. My husband was always very interested in India."

As Lucien's mystified face disappeared in clouds of steam from under the wheel and the train pulled away toward York, she called, "You must come and stay with us."

"Oh, Ma," groaned Seb.

"Well, of course he must. Your father was very fond of Indians."

"He's not an Indian."

133

"But I thought it was a Buddhist—"

"No, it wasn't and he's not. He's Jewish, actually."

"Now, your father was very interested in the Jews. You know, I don't think we ever met any *Jewish* Indians."

"Ma!" Seb looked down at the crown of her felt hat. "I didn't think we had anywhere to ask anyone to stay."

"Don't be too sure of that," she said, looking up and smiling. She presented her ticket as if it were a prize, and the two men discussed whether or not she was an actress slowly throughout the afternoon.

They were unable, however, to give any news of the people who were to be gathering to meet her, and it was with some relief that Mrs. Price spotted Posie's chauffeur at last coming toward them. "We're going back with Posie," she said to Seb. "Yes, all of us. Home with her to Scarborough. Not for long. There are *great* news—oh, look, there's Dr. Padshaw and Beams. Hoo!" she called, lifting her arms as Dr. Padshaw's bulk thudded down from his truck, followed by Beams in a ragged jersey and showing her knickers. "And there's Sybil Thing," said Seb, "with that funny woman. And someone else."

"We all had to come," said Sybil sadly, "because of dear Athie's luggage. *I* can't lift it and I wasn't sure that there'd be anyone here to help Primmy. You know Primrose, don't you? This is Winnie from the Cook's Cove Hotel."

"How lovely." Mrs. Price clasped her hands. "This is my daughter Phoebe and—oh, I'm sorry—Dr. Padshaw. Let's go and see Posie in her car. Dr. Padshaw, how very good of you to bring Phoebe all the way from—er."

"Pleasure," said Dr. Padshaw, which was not how he had been regarding the eternal silence, with Beams handkerchief-sucking beside him, the past two hours.

"Everyone here but Mim. Hello, Posie—oh, Posie dear, how lovely. All one's dearest friends. All here. It's just like the— How good people are. What *about* Mim's luggage, Sybil? Surely you haven't still got Mim's luggage?"

"We've been—er—just hanging on to it," said Sybil.

"Yes, she went off without it," said Primrose and got back into the car and began to read *Country Life.*

"Dear me . . ."

"Tek no notice," said Winnie. "You and me'll shift it, eh?" She looked at Beams, but kind Dr. Padshaw took charge and the cases were lifted out of Sybil's boot and presented to Posie's chauffeur. "They'll be quite light now," said Mrs. Price, "without the presents. What about the rope ladder? Did she take it loose?"

"I—er—believe she left it with a friend," said Sybil.

"In a bit of a two-an'-eight," announced Winnie.

"Who? Athene?" said Mrs. Price.

"That's right. She needs looking after, that one."

"Athene? My elder daughter? But she's quite the kingpin of us all."

"Fine girl," boomed Dr. Padshaw, who had seen her once.

"She *does* get in a two-and-eight," said Beams, and moved nearer Winnie, examining her with respect.

"But where has she gone?" called Posie from the car. "Where *is* Athie?"

"They're late," said Mrs. Price. "Dear me, half an hour late. It's probably that car of Boo's."

But it was not, for Boo's car was at that moment seen coming slowly up the station approach and Boo getting briskly out alone. "Hello," she called, carefully locking all the doors, pulling down the jacket of her uniform, straightening her shoulders. "Is she here?"

135

"Who? Here?" asked Mrs. Price.

"Theeny? Is she here?"

"No. Of course not. She's with you."

"Oh, dear," said Boo. "Where has she got to? She *was* with me. She's disappeared."

"Oh, she'll be here in a minute," said Seb.

"Did you stop or something?"

"Well, yes—just as we got into Darlington she remembered some apple pie or something from that shop in Skinnergate. Said you'd told her to get one for Posie, Dodo. She just shouted 'Stop' and jumped out and disappeared. I waited and waited, but you can't stop long in Skinnergate, it's so narrow, and in the end I got out and went after her and they'd never seen her."

"Who hadn't?"

"In the shop. Said nobody had been in for half an hour. A pretty girl, I said. I said they'd remember her. They said nobody."

"She probably couldn't find the shop once she was out," said Dr. Padshaw. "She'll be here in a minute." They stood talking for a while and Seb began to ask about sailing, which started a conversation threatening to last some hours.

"I think perhaps we ought to start to search about a bit," said Mrs. Price. "Is there another entrance to the station?"

This was examined, but no girl stood waiting.

"We'd better go back to Skinnergate. Look here," said Dr. Padshaw to the chauffeur, "I'll find this Skinnergate and you just coast round the town a bit. Take this chap." Seb was put into the Daimler and Posie brought out of it and deposited in the station tea room, where she ate a meat pie at a table ringed with beer. The cars moved off, searched, and in half an hour were back. There had been so sign of Athene.

"This is very silly," said Mrs. Price.

"Very," said Primrose, flicking pages. "Though nothing new."

"Perhaps—"

"She may have had a lapse of memory," said Beams. "A blockage."

"Blockage, eh?" laughed Dr. Padshaw, but stopped.

"How has she been, Boo?"

"Well, I simply don't know. I only saw her last night, you know. Just arrived."

"What! *Athene* just arrived?"

"I'm simply not clear. I think she'd been camping, rather."

"Camping?"

"Well, my flat was locked. I told you I'd be on the course till—"

"You mean she has been alone since—"

"Well, she can't have been alone for long. I mean, she's only just left Sybil's."

Sybil opened her mouth and then helplessly shut it again.

"So you have muddled it, Boo."

"How can I muddle other people's arrangements? Nobody has been able to get in touch with you. I have a life too, Dodo, though it always escaped your attention."

Seb said quickly that they ought perhaps to have a look round again, and Primrose snapped from the car that someone might like to go to the police station.

"Or the hospitals," said Sybil. "She may have had an accident."

"Or run away," said Posie, with a bright smile.

"Run away?" Mrs. Price was brisk. "Posie, what are you talking about?"

"She might," said Beams, considering.

"How was she, anyway?" Sebastian asked Boo.

"Oh, well, she was . . . Actually, she was very quiet. But she always is quiet, bless her. Perhaps she was extra quiet—and she looked, well, rather worn, I thought. Yes, she did look rather worn when she came out of the woods. She wasn't in when I got back. That nice fellow Bell had been about and she'd been for a walk with him."

"God!" said Seb.

"She didn't eat supper. Yes—she went to bed early. I was busy unpacking and reading all your letters, Dodo, and sorting them out. She didn't want breakfast either. She had a headache in the car. I think she fell asleep on the way here, as a matter of fact. Not a word out of her."

"And then she jumped out of your car and ran away," said Mrs. Price. "How very efficient your Red Cross activities have made you."

"We have wasted nearly an hour," Dr. Padshaw said loudly. "It sounds as if the girl has disappeared. I think we must go to the police."

Beams said suddenly and vehemently, "No."

"But where is she?" Sybil wailed, and Primrose looked at her watch. "I mean, where would she go?"

Winnie said, "Well, she's about seventeen, en't she? En't she all of seventeen?"

"What has that to do with it?"

"Well, seems to me she's older than you all think. She's probably made her own plans."

"Own plans! My dear woman," said Mrs. Price, "she is still a schoolgirl."

"Her own plans," said Winnie. "Seems likely to me that she's probably just gone 'ome."

Chapter Twenty-one

The wide drive of the rectory was thick with weeds now almost to the middle, the sexton jabbing about at them dolefully with a rake as the first car approached. He stopped, wandered to the white gate and, seeing Sebastian in the truck, began to ease it open. It had always been difficult. Now it shrieked.

The house itself had sad, dark windows downstairs. Upstairs all was shuttered. A great overblown rose had come right off the wall and hung drunkenly outward in a hoop. Leaves had drifted against the steps of the french windows. A shutter clattered.

"He's been an' he's gone again," said the sexton to Sebastian as he jumped down onto the weeds. "A real high flier. A real whizzbanger. Incense. Ten candles. Made-to-measure vestments. No wife. God help us."

"*Gone* again?" said Seb.

"Aye—back next week in residence. Looking for a house-keeper. Fast car. Tooken all the vestry keys."

"We're actually looking for Athie."

"Times have changed. God help us."

"You haven't seen her, have you? It just occurred to us she might have come back here."

"Wish we had your mother back here. Look at yon roses. Look at them surplices. No choir laundry since the day His Reverence died."

Dr. Padshaw, who had been hurrying round the house, came back toward them. "All seems firmly locked there," he said. "No signs of anyone. Bolted and barred."

"She might be in the barn," said Seb.

"If you saw them surplices. Or rather if your mother saw them surplices. Not that anyone can see any surplices, all the vestry keys being tooken. Filthy, torn lace. Mice. God help us. He's importing a ciborium. 'An' what's a ciborium?' I asks. 'If it's silver you can tek it back. Mrs. Arrowsmith's willing, but she's not Mrs. Price,' I says, 'and I'm not even sure if Mrs. Price would have stood for a ciborium.' "

"Church is locked up too," said Dr. Padshaw. The sexton stopped talking for a moment to consider the march of time and Dr. Padshaw and Sebastian stood by him in the empty garden feeling rather foolish. A roaring behind them in the lane announced the arrival of Primrose's Austin, and behind slid up the Daimler.

"Here's Mother if you want to talk to her," said Seb.

Wandering off with his rake, the sexton called back to them, "The west door's open any road, ten candles or no. The old Rector wouldn't have it locked, and locked it won't be in my time."

"Well, it's locked now," said Dr. Padshaw.

140

It was. First Seb tried it, then his mother, then Beams, then Dr. Padshaw again. Finally the sexton tried. "Aye—it's locked," he said. "From inside an' all. Mebbe it's Athie."

"Athie!"

"Aye—she went inside."

"Good God—when?"

"About half an hour since. Drifting by. Mind when she seest state ont you'd think she'd want nothing with stopping. Fit to make you drop offt tower."

Uneasily and as if by some silent command they all looked upward at the tower high above, above even the treetops, dark against the pale September sky, fast clouds over it.

They rattled the door again. It was heavy, of Tudor oak, black as iron. Mrs. Price borrowed Posie's umbrella and rapped at a window, loosening John the Baptist.

"Tek care now, Mrs. P," said the sexton. "Things is bad enough."

"Athie!" they called. "At!" "Theeny!" "Darling!" "Mim!"

"ATHENE!" bellowed Dr. Padshaw, filling his lungs. The chauffeur, who had moved away in embarrassment to stand beside the gate, gave a sudden yelp, and pointed.

They stood back and saw her—or what must be her—a dark droop leaning against the flagpole attached to the corner of the tower that faced the rectory. She held the pole with both hands and her head was thoughtfully bowed on her chest. She swung there a little toward them and the wind that was flinging the clouds across the sky far above her took the rope of the flagpole and swelled it outward in an arc and pulled out her hair into a strip behind her.

"She's like a figurehead," said Beams.

"My God, she's going to jump," cried the chauffeur, and Dr. Padshaw gathered a great gulp of air into his lungs and

141

bellowed "ATHENE!" again. With a clatter, Boo's car arrived in the lane and she got out, having first wiped over the inside of the windscreen. After a minute she leaned back into the car and brought out some binoculars. She hesitated with them in her hands a moment, then put them back.

Those at the foot of the tower were now in a circle holding Posie's mohair car rug. They began a sort of agitated dance: Dr. Padshaw, the chauffeur, Primrose, Sybil hobbling, the sexton half-hearted ("Athie's big-boned. She'd go right through"), and Beams and Boo and Sebastian. Posie and Winnie moved away and stood side by side under the lych gate like fat pawns out of the game. Mrs. Price with short quick steps moved away round the corner too and sat with her back to everybody on top of a flat tombstone. "Steady now," cried Dr. Padshaw as Athene leaned further. Primrose Clarke began a horrible wailing.

But it was Beams whose nerve broke. Unusually childish, arms and legs awry, back hunched, she ran at her mother, shouting.

"She's looking at the graves. Ma, she's looking at the grave! It's not good for her!"

Her mother turned away her face, her chin drawn down.

"It's all bulged up and the flowers are dead and the turfs are cracking!"

Mrs. Price did not stir. Beams flew on, rushed to the lych gate and hid her face in Posie's sloping chest.

Seb appeared round the tower and yelled, "Do something! She's going to jump!" and rushed back. Beams turned and shouted again, "She's going to jump! Go to her! Shout at her! She's going to die!"

"She'll not jump," said Winnie.

"She's going to jump."

142

"She'll not jump," said Posie.

Seb yelled again.

"She'll not jump," said Mrs. Price at last. "Athene's well taught."

Primrose came shouting in a rolling, uncontrolled, sickening voice about the fire brigade. "Someone—send someone! Send those people at the gate!" (For the village had gathered.)

"Send for the police!" shouted Boo. "It is a suicide."

Mrs. Price lifted her head and took out her fountain pen. "A note," she said, "under the door. Who knows? Prayer first, then sensible action."

But there was a great gust of wind, a thudding of feet and Seb's wild cry, "She's down! She's down!"

Beams ran from Posie and crouched at her mother's feet, putting her handkerchief in her mouth and closing her eyes.

Chapter Twenty-two

To Athene the cry "ATHENE!" came up like an echo of such a cry or the memory of it, but she opened her eyes. Birds sailed beneath her, tattered rooks at untidy angles in the wind. Pale ovals looked at her far below like steppingstones in the grass. She saw rooks' nests in the treetops, to her right the harsh pattern of haphazard graves.

She swung inward, let go of the post and settled onto the smooth, warm roof, that rose to a blunt point in the middle, ribbed with seams of lead. She examined the construction of the roof carefully. There was a neat channel all round for rainwater, a hole in each corner revealing the gaping mouth of a drainpipe. The top of each drainpipe supported a little box decorated with lead leaves and flowers. Someone—some Elizabethan or someone—must have done them. Had he done them up here or on the ground? Well, on the ground, of course. You couldn't mold lead oak leaves up here. Not in a wind. You'd be swept off. You'd have a scaffolding perhaps. Did Elizabethans have scaffolding? Her father would know.

How funny. Perhaps he had never seen the boxes. Or the channels on the lead roof. What a shame. He would have liked it up here. In the wind. With all the shouting and the graves and the fuss far away.

I must look at the graveyard.

Instead she leaned back against the sloping lead and looked at the sky.

I must look at the graveyard.

She sat up, climbed on all fours over the pointed roof and looked down at the other side of the tower. In a moment there was a sort of flurry below and the pink ovals appeared there, too. Again a sort of murmur came up to her. The ovals were in a ring now and holding something, some carpet sort of thing. They looked like pink stones holding down a picnic cloth in a breeze. No, they didn't. They looked like people holding something in a circle in their outstretched hands.

"They think I'm going to jump," she thought, astonished. "Goodness, and I didn't know."

Thoughtful still, she made her way round the drain to the north side of the tower and looked directly at the graveyard. "I must look at the graveyard," she said, and, taking hold of two stone castellations, an arm lovingly round each, she hitched herself up and leaned outward—very far.

"There," she said triumphantly. "There." In the noisy, plucking wind her eye was caught by a flash below—Beams' glasses and the ungainly blob that was Beams scuttling like a brown beetle desperately round the tower and away.

The dancers were there again, shuffling round until they were directly below her, the ovals like pink beads. They were like the net you put over milk with beads sewn round the edge

145

to weight it down. Pretty things to make. You see them still in Scotland.

Beams had gone, awry and wild, but after a time so weird and long it seemed no time at all, Athene, opening the church door, saw her again, crouched by a tombstone, and her mother writing. As she opened the church door wider a great gust of wind battered the rectory wall behind them and she saw the poor rose totter there and fall. She heard Seb cry, "She's down! She's down!" saw her mother begin to screw up her pen, touch Beams' shoulder, saying, "Look, child, look."

Then she saw the unlikely company trooping forward over the grass, some hurrying, some hanging back. They were motley, heavy, not beautiful, with gaping faces. She saw them as if she had come down from the moon and had never seen people before. Trailing the rug these plain people came, all thinking only about her.

"Why should they?" she thought. "Why ever should they?" Her face, dirty and streaked and wan, fell sideways, her mouth became a cave and she began to weep before them all.

"There now," said Boo. "A breakdown!"

But "Breakdown me eye," said Winnie, tramping forward. "She'll be grand. She'll be grand directly."

Chapter Twenty-three

My dearest Posie,

You will think me very foolish writing to you already for Christmas but we are so very busy that I have to slip in letters where I can and this evening the students are being unusually self-reliant and I seem to have my sitting room to myself.

Well—I am thoroughly enjoying being a housekeeper. I seem perfectly able to do the work and am changing a great many things which I think will be to everyone's advantage. Poor Mabel Palethorpe has gone, which is perhaps as well, and I am in complete charge.

I wonder if you have heard that I have Athene with me? Seb and Phoebe are back at school (trust funds) but darling Mim decided that she no longer cared for hers. In fact there was

147

absolutely no discussing the matter with her. She more or less enrolled herself at the local high school (very odd children with curious low brows) and then informed me about it. She has also cut off her hair. It is quite straight all round with a fringe like Joan of Arc. She is much changed. Seldom plays the piano and then in quite a different way, has dropped the Classics and—now, Posie dear, be prepared—has begun to take a great interest in Politics, and rather on the left-hand side. She seems to read nothing pleasant at all. Really I sometimes wonder if I know her any more. She marches about the house and has taken to speaking her mind and I do sometimes—but this is entirely between ourselves—wonder if she might not grow a bit like Boo. It is a very upsetting thought. Though I can't honestly say that she has lost her looks. She is just quite different.

Really too it was Mim (By the way, she won't have Mim any more. Or Athene either. She has told them at this school that her name is Anna. Personally I find this Bolshevik)—it was Mim who made the decision about coming here. My great news—that you never heard, my dear Posie, after that dreadful day—my news was that we had been offered a chance of going home. Yes. I heard a few days before we all met at Darlington. The new rector of Newton is a bachelor not expected to marry (high) and needing a housekeeper. I was asked if we would like to move back.

I couldn't tell you at Scarborough the week when you took us all in, and where we should have been without you I ask myself daily. That week I felt no. I must choose my moment, so when we came on here to Mabel Palethorpe's and Athene was better—she was very odd, you know—I told them then.

Life is full of surprises and I had three. Sebastian said,

"What? Go back? To the rectory?" in the most scandalized way. Phoebe said in that silly psychiatrist voice she puts on—though we are hearing less of it since she decided that she wants to be a journalist—that she thought it would be "highly dangerous," and *Mim* looked across at me quite sharply and said, "Oh, Mother. Really!"

I said—I think that is the only time that I have felt anger since Alfred left us—"*Well*, Athene, I suppose you realize that the alternative is here?"

"What here?" said Sebastian. "Manchester?"

"Yes," I said, "Mabel Palethorpe has a proposition."

He said something that was rather unkind and asked if Mabel Palethorpe would be here too and I said I felt not for long. "Good," he said, and "Might as well," said Beams, "fine." Mim if you please—yes, *Mim*, dear—said she thought it was a splendid idea and Manchester might make us all a bit less fancy. It was then that I had the awful presentiment that she might get like Boo.

Well, I can't get used to the people, but there is much Christian work to be done and it is really very nice having Mim at home. I find that I do very much look forward to her step upon the stairs. This is something I have not before experienced and it is I suppose one of the greatest joys in a *much diminished* life. Oddly too, although Mim is so different and sometimes ominous and does make some very bewildering remarks—and mind I would never have said this to Alfred—I must admit that she is a lot more *fun* than she ever was. Really a bit more my sort.

Our Christmas is going to be very quiet. Sebastian is bringing home a foreign boy who has something or other to do with Crag Foot—a small world. Beams is going of all places to

149

a washing-up job at that deadly Cook's Cove hotel. She wants to study Cook's Cove, she says—I suppose, fossils or something. Sebastian is off in January to those nice Padshaws sailing, though I can't think it will be suitable weather.

I hear you are going to Harrogate this Christmas. How is Doris Messenger? I wonder now if you will still be at Scarborough about December 15th? If so I can get Sybil to drop you in an Ellison's pie from Redcar on her way to that sensible Primrose. I hear by the way that Sybil is going for drives with some *artist!!* Poor fellow. The pie would be no distance for them (30 miles?) and always makes a nice present. Let me know, dear, for I shall have to get Sybil well prepared and send her the Postal Order. She is as great a muddler as poor Boo.

I don't suppose I shall ever hear exactly what went wrong with them both this summer. Do you know, Sybil has not said *one word* about the crucifix! There is something which I simply cannot tell you about Boo and some binoculars. A very expensive rope ladder also disappeared. Boo and I as a matter of fact are still not writing.

However, these are details. What matters is that my darling Mim had a restful, quiet summer. Without you all how much worse her upset might have been. You know, I really think between ourselves that what Mim wants . . .

And she wrote on. Athene, swinging into the room, taller now, a bit sharper round the nose, dropped her books onto a chair and watched her. "One moment," her mother said, pen racing. "Posie. Just finishing. One keeps writing. Goodness knows how much she takes in. By the way, I forgot to tell you, Sebastian has invited a very nice young Jewish Indian for Christmas. A Jewish Buddhist, from Edinburgh.

150

"Well, what's the matter?" she asked, wielding blotting paper. "What are you laughing at now?"

"I don't know," said Athene, laughing more. Rosy from the Manchester drizzle, she said, "Oh, Ma, I love you. Keep going. I'll get the tea."